YA MOORE
Moore, Stephanie Perry.
Better than picture perfect /

Better Than
Picture Perfect

THE **SHARP** SISTERS

#2

Better Than Picture Perfect

STEPHANIE PERRY MOORE

darby creek
MINNEAPOLIS

Darby Creek
A division of Lerner Publishing Group, Inc.
241 First Avenue North
Minneapolis, MN 55401 USA

For reading levels and more information, look up this title at
www.lernerbooks.com.

The images in this book are used with the permission of:
Front Cover: © Andreas Kuehn/Iconica/Getty Images;
© SeanPavonePhoto/Shutterstock.com, (background).

Main body text set in Janson Text LT Std 12/17.5.
Typeface provided by Linotype AG.

Library of Congress Cataloging-in-Publication Data

Moore, Stephanie Perry.
        Better than picture perfect / Stephanie Perry Moore.
            pages   cm. — (The Sharp sisters)
        Summary: Seventeen-year-old aspiring photographer Ansli Sharp,
    the adopted daughter of a mayoral candidate, learns that her
    boyfriend is one of the twenty homeless students in her school and
    decides to reach out to them.
        ISBN 978-1-4677-3725-8 (lib. bdg. : alk. paper)
        ISBN 978-1-4677-4655-7 (eBook)
        [1. Homeless persons—Fiction. 2. High schools—Fiction. 3. Schools—
    Fiction. 4. Dating (Social customs)—Fiction. 5. Orphans—Fiction.
    6. Adoption—Fiction.] I. Title.
    PZ7.M788125Bet 2014
    [Fic]—dc23   2013040857

Manufactured in the United States of America
1 – SB – 7/15/14

For
Tyra Banks

You are a sister I admire.
Thank you for teaching young people
how to be gorgeous on the inside
and out.
I love how you pursued your dream
at a young age and turned it into an
empire.
May every person reading this series
strive to be dynamic like you.

You show us how to capture
perfection. Glad your life inspires
others … proud of you!

CHAPTER ONE
AUDACITY

It's interesting when the world looks at you and thinks you have it going on, but the way you see yourself is anything but. Not a day goes by without somebody commenting on my looks. "Oooh your honey, tanned-yellow skin is perfect." "I wish I had your silky, Indian-type hair." "Mixed people are the most beautiful on earth." While those comments are always flattering, they don't do anything to uplift my spirit.

It's hard being me. Though I'm a part of a family most would envy, it is tough keeping up with the Sharps, even if you are one. My father is running for mayor of the city of Charlotte for goodness sake. We are in the spotlight, and I'm tired of the brightness.

My parents work hard and do well. They are lawyers who had a good start because my dad was an NFL player. Money is not a scarcity. I'm just seventeen, but I've learned money isn't everything, and it certainly can't buy you happiness.

See, my parents aren't my parents, and three out of four of my sisters aren't really my biological sisters. Sometimes I feel the love and affection they try to give is really pity. My real parents were taken from me and my younger sister, Yuri, at a young age. I don't know all the details, but I know a plane went down, and they were on it. No survivors. My biological mom was from England, and her parents are still alive, but the decision was made to keep me and my little sister with my dad's best friend and his wife.

All I've ever known was Stanley and Sherri Sharp as my parents. My first memory of a friend is playing with Shelby, their oldest daughter, and she's never left my side. In the beginning, everything was cool, but in these most recent years as a teenager, I've been struggling.

I'm a senior in high school. I'm about to go out on my own and find my way in the world. However, how can I discover that if I truly don't even know who I am? The big question mark is: where have I come from? And while I sat in the posh restaurant next door to a big fashion show that's just taken place to celebrate Shelby's debut as a designer, I was a little jealous.

"Do you hear me?" my rude sister Sloan interrupted.

She was the baby of the original Sharp girls. The other two I admired. Shelby was truly outgoing. Slade dreamed of stardom day and night and thought she was going to be the next Beyoncé or Rihanna. Sloan was irritating and had no regard as to how she said things.

"I didn't hear you," I turned around and said.

Exasperated, Sloan voiced, "Well, I've only been calling your name for hours."

"Girl, we ain't even been in here for hours," Yuri, my biological sister who was the same age as Sloan, quickly stepped up and said.

It meant a lot that Yuri would defend me. She was shy. Maybe because Yuri and Sloan were the same age they could relate to each other better.

"What do you want?" I said to Sloan now that she had my attention.

"For you to pass the menu. When Mom, Dad, and Shelby come, the three of us want to be ready to order, dang," Sloan uttered.

"Yeah, we haven't been here for hours, but the four of us have definitely been sitting here for thirty minutes or so," Slade looked at her watch and commented like she had somewhere to go. "A new television show is coming on I gotta see. Just pick something, Ansli."

Suddenly the quiet restaurant became full of excitement as the press and paparazzi entered, snapping pictures. It seemed like the president himself was entering, but it was just my parents and Shelby. I wasn't upset that she was getting a lot of attention. She truly deserved it. She is so talented, and I love her dearly. The green-eyed monster within me was beginning to shine because I felt that I had no talent to develop like she did. Instead of being a sourpuss I grabbed my Nikon, walked toward the door, and started taking my own pictures. One of the professional photographers did a double take at my camera and lens. While most people were satisfied with taking pictures on their low-end cameras, to me, there was still nothing like using the finest equipment to get the best images.

Shelby came right over to me and gave me a big hug. I was supposed to be taking pictures, and here she was hugging me. "It was so great, Ansli! I hate you weren't there."

"Me too," I told her honestly. "Snag me a ticket next time."

The fashion show she did for up-and-coming designer Sydnee Sheldon was a ticketed event. They only gave her passes for our parents. I knew she'd tell me all about it just like I was there. She tugged on my hand, pulled me closer to her, and said, "Spencer was there, and he asked me to be his girl."

We both screamed until we noticed our parents looking over at us like, "settle down."

Reporters started asking her a few questions. I saw her inner glow about Spencer and thought of my guy. I started texting Hugo.

Hugo Green was a Hispanic hunk that I'd been talking to over the summer and for the first few weeks of school. Usually he texted me right back. Maybe his phone was off, battery was dead, or something because, even if he was busy, he usually got back to me as soon as possible. However, he wasn't texting back, and I didn't even realize how much I'd grown to depend on him to give me an uplifting word when I felt down in the dumps. Lately, I wasn't feeling like I belonged to the Sharp family. We're supposed to be acting like we're the closest family on earth, and while we were close, something still seemed off.

"What? Do y'all think you all are special or something?" Mr. Brown, one of my dad's opponents, obnoxiously said as he tried coming into the restaurant. "Where's the manager? Get these people away from the door. You can't even take in any new customers."

People cleared the way to let him through. He was such a jerk. He looked to be about fifty and had a shiny bald head with a bunch of lumps on top of it. It seemed like he was almost 250 pounds, and his suit was too small. When he breathed, it looked like he was going to pop a button. Yet, there he stood, thinking he was all that.

"Sharp, what's up best friend?" Brown sneered.

My dad just laughed.

"Oh what? You think just because you clowned me next door and called me out on domestic violence you're better than me?"

"I didn't say anything about the allegations your wife made on you publicly about domestic violence. Let's be clear," my dad responded, clearly wanting to escort us to our seats in order to not cause a scene. But he had to reply because he wasn't Brown's punk.

Mr. Brown stepped in his face. "Yeah, whatever. You act like you're so appalled

"Oh, you think I'm not?"

"Well, you shouldn't be so naive. After all, those two girls you adopted became yours when their dad took a shotgun and shot his wife and himself. If that ain't domestic violence, I don't know what is. And you're raising his kids, telling the world they are your best friend's girls," Mr. Brown stated, almost daring my dad to refute it.

At that moment, the camera I cared so deeply for fell right out of my hands.

***

"You're a liar!" I screamed, tired of being timid and allowing crazy adults to determine how I act and feel.

"Ansli!" my mom shouted like she was disappointed in me, as if I'd done something unladylike.

Honestly, I didn't care anymore. The cameras were rolling, but I wasn't going to have this fool saying anything to get attention to win a dumb election and soil the memory I had of my folks in the process. If adults couldn't check him, I was going to.

"Just go, Brown," my dad quickly said, trying to hug me.

"Oh no, no, no. You're daughter thinks *I'm* a liar?" Mr. Brown said as he tried to touch my shoulder. "Ask your dad if I'm telling the truth. I'm surprised you believed everything he said. Heck, you're a teenager. Y'all all over the Internet these days. You ain't checked the facts? You ain't read up on it? You ain't seen whose names was on the flight that went down over the Everglades that he claims that your parents were on? Anyone who lies like that to their own children who they profess to love shouldn't be running no city."

"Man, get out of here! You're just trying to turn this into a circus!" my dad yelled.

"You're the clown, man. Ask your dad if it's true. What? Cat's got your tongue? You ain't asking him," Mr. Brown drilled me.

My mother's eyes were watering. Though my dad always had his composure, he was shaking. Shelby looked so disappointed. Every sad emotion that was coming across her face was how I felt inside, but add rage to it, and that would define me.

"How dare you lie to me all of my life?! I hate you! I hate you!" I shouted out as loud as I could to my folks, still feeling that wasn't even loud enough.

I had to go tell Yuri. She had to know the truth. Though she wasn't as old as me, we were only two years apart. She was a sophomore in high school, and she deserved to know the truth as well.

As I took off to finagle through the restaurant to go speak to my sister, Shelby followed. "Come on, sis! There's got to be an explanation. You've got to calm down. You can't just believe that man."

"You saw our parents. Did they deny it? They were looking straight in my eyes. They had ever opportunity to clear up this so-called misunderstanding, but they couldn't. You know why they couldn't, Shelby? Because they've been feeding me garbage for years. Well, I'm tired of being a charity case."

"Mr. Brown is just trying to make Dad look bad," Shelby insisted.

"When you do something bad, no one has to make you look any other way than what you actually look like. Let's keep it real, Shelby. Did Dad take me and Yuri in all these years because he wanted the voters' sympathy?"

"That's ridiculous. You're talking stupid now."

"Yeah, but you better watch out because I just found out my dad shot my mom, and I might have terrible anger streaks in me." I jerked my hand away from her. I went up to my sister.

"Yuri, Yuri! Come on. We've got to go."

"What do you mean? We haven't even eaten. We just ordered my favorites," my true sister yelled out, unsure why I was acting like such maniac.

I tried to get her up, but she wouldn't move. Dad had broken my heart, and the last thing I wanted to do was break Slade's and Sloan's. They thought their parents could do no wrong, or knew best, but that wasn't the case. If my sister wouldn't move for me to tell her in private, then all three of them were going to find out.

"What? What's the problem?" Sloan said, seeing the harsh look in my eye.

"Yuri, let's go," I said, ignoring Sloan as soon as my parents walked toward the table.

"Why?" Yuri asked.

"Because these folks aren't who we think they are okay?" I blurted out.

Yuri's face cringed, like she had just tasted something nasty. "What are you talking about?"

My mom came over and said, "Ansli, please not now. Let us tell her our own way".

Insulted, I huffed, "What? Like you told me?"

"Tell me what?" Yuri said, looking confused.

"Yeah, tell her what?" Slade demanded to know.

"You're acting like we never knew we were adopted," Yuri said.

"I mean they're not the parents we thought they were. It's all been a lie."

My dad got to the table and said, "Alright, Ansli. That's enough."

"Don't tell me what to do!" I shouted.

"Ansli!" Yuri said, completely disgusted at how I was responding.

"What happened to your parents, Yuri? What happened to your biological parents? Why are they not here?" I asked my sister.

"You know why. They were in a plane crash

years ago," Yuri told me wincing as she recalled the unpleasant life-changing information.

Schooling her, I bellowed, "No, your dad took a gun and killed your mom and then killed himself. Heck, if we were in the house, he might have killed us too!"

Mom reached over and back-slapped me. I held my face. All my sisters' mouths hung open so wide a fist could fit into them.

As my eyes teared up, my mom said, "I'm so sorry, Ansli. I'm so sorry! I just . . . I just . . . "

Cutting her off I bawled, "What? You're just showing me how you really feel about me? Your real daughter Sloan gets smart all the time, and you never say anything, but when I tell the truth you're going to hit me in the mouth?"

"Come on girls, let's go," my dad said to us, after he handed the waiter who was eavesdropping a large bill.

"Are you kidding? The last place I'm going is home with you guys," I bluntly told him, rolling my eyes as I headed out.

"Ansli, wait!" my mom called out like she cared. After she just burned my face with her

hand, I was through. I had pain on the inside
and out.

**

"Taxi!" I yelled when I got out to the curb.

When the first one passed me by, I put my
hand in my mouth and whistled, then the second yellow car I saw stopped.

"Where to, ma'am?" the young, scrappy,
red-headed driver turned around and asked.

Still fuming, I uttered, "Can't you just drive
straight until I tell you to turn?" Why did everyone want me to comply with their rules? Why
did I have to surrender to their way of thinking?
How come I always was pressured to do things
their way? Not anymore.

"Okay, your dime," the driver said, seeing I
wasn't in a good mood. "But if you tell me where
you want to go I might be able get you there
faster and save you some money, but you ain't
got to tell me twice."

Where was I going to go? My parents had
done a great job of providing a roof over my
head—or maybe I should call them the Sharps

because I just didn't feel that parent-child thing any longer. Thinking of them made me ill, like I had the flu and it was turning into pneumonia. I looked at my phone and realized Hugo had not texted me back. I needed to see him. I needed him to wrap his strong arms around me. His 210-pound frame was fine. Although he wasn't an athlete, he was more fit than most athletes I knew. Now that I was going through this, having him hold me or maybe even taking our relationship to the next level would be the only thing that could set my upside-down world back right side up.

I checked one of my earlier emails when we first started talking, and I remembered asking him where he lived, and he'd actually given me his address. It wasn't like him not to respond to me. I was sure the way he'd been pressuring me hard for sex and had been feeling a girl up, if he was going through anything, maybe we could cheer each other up by getting busy. So, if I popped by, I couldn't see that being a bad thing, particularly since I was going through a crisis.

"Great! There it is," I screeched as I found the address. "Go to 3411 South Watermill Road."

"You're going over there?" The taxicab driver said with disdain.

"Yeah, why?"

"It's just a different side of town from where I picked you up. Just making sure you know where you're going. There's some Hispanic gangs over there, and I'm just looking out for a pretty girl. That's all."

"Well, I don't need you all up in my business," I said to the carrot top, scary-looking driver.

Later we pulled into Waters Edge, the name of the complex that looked like it needed to be condemned. I started feeling a little uneasy. I was dressed up. If I was going to meet Hugo's family, I didn't want them to think I was full of myself. I didn't wear a lot of name brand stuff to school. Not because I wasn't proud to wear the clothes, I just was conscious that everyone wasn't fortunate, and flaunting around what my parents—or should I say Shelby's parents—could afford didn't seem right.

"Last time I came over here, some guys tried to jump me and take my little cash, so I've got to let you out here, senorita. You're on your own," the driver said, being an obnoxious, smart guy.

I didn't appreciate his tone or the racial profiling. Yeah, he was a white guy in a high-end cab, and one time he'd been in a Hispanic neighborhood, and probably not even this one, where he'd gotten jacked. However, that didn't mean it was going to happen again, but whatever. I just opened the door, paid him his money, and started walking.

As soon as he sped away, I panicked, wondering how in the world was I going to get home? I didn't get the cab driver's cell number for him to come pick me up again. Not like I wanted to get in his car again anyway, but still the option was gone, and I knew Hugo didn't have a car. Maybe his mother did, but on the real, it wasn't like I wanted to go home anyway.

My phone started ringing. I clicked it off so I didn't have to hear it, but soon it started up again. I looked at the phone, and it was Shelby's number. I knew if I didn't answer it, she wouldn't stop calling. She was persistent that way.

"Yes? What?" I said.

"You've got Mom and Dad worried like crazy. Where are you? We saw you getting into that cab, but we have no idea where you went. Do you have money to pay?"

"I'm fine. You don't have to worry about me, and I'm not coming home tonight."

"Dagon-it, Ansli! You are coming home! Let's just talk about this. Where are you?"

When I reached Hugo's door and saw a sign that read, "Eviction Notice," and a big padlock prohibiting someone from entering, I said, "I've got to go, Shelby. I'll talk to you later."

"Don't hang up!" she begged.

But I hung up. What in the world happened to Hugo? What was going on? What was up? There was no need to bang on the door. The blinds were up, and I could see through the window that the place looked deserted.

"That family is down the street at the shelter," this older African-American lady using a cane said.

"Ma'am? Are you sure? My boyfriend lives here."

The woman sized me up and must have decided I was a decent girl because she began talking to me. "He's in the shelter with his momma and his cute little brother. That nice young man you're calling your boyfriend done went up there to that homeless shelter. I felt so bad for him. I would've let him live here with me if my grown kids didn't have to stay here. That landlord knows he could have given that woman more time to find a job, but he said after four months without no pay he couldn't do it no mo'."

She pointed me in the direction of the homeless shelter, and every step I walked, I felt even sicker than I had before, like I needed to be on a ventilator or something. Life in me was just gone. Hugo, his mom and little brother homeless? It just wasn't right.

When I got to the homeless shelter it was closed. There was a big sign on the door that said, "Come back tomorrow. You must be here by seven o'clock to get in." Now it was nine, but I didn't want to stay.

Actually, I needed to stay. I didn't have a place to go either. I just wanted to talk to Hugo. Maybe if the two of us got away, we could figure this thing out. So I rang the doorbell and pounded on the door until someone came.

"Can you read young lady?" a plump, older, blond-headed woman said to me.

"I'm sorry I'm not here to come in. I need to speak with Hugo Green. Please, please."

She opened the door a little farther, and there he was holding his little brother's hand.

"Go on with Mom," Hugo tapped the little boy and said.

"Thank you, ma'am," I said.

Hugo came to the door and said, "Can I just speak with her for a second? For her to be all the way here, something has got to be wrong."

"Okay, but we can't take anybody else," she told him.

"Her dad's running for mayor, she wouldn't need to stay here," he laughed and said.

The woman's whole demeanor became nicer. "Oh my gosh! I thought you looked familiar. Well, go on out. The last thing I want you to do is report that things aren't great here. I've seen your dad with all the state officials, even the director of my center. Take all the time you need. Just come around to the back door. I'll leave that open for you."

"Why'd you tell her about my dad?" I scolded him when we were alone.

"Why'd you track me down here? You've been texting me. I hadn't replied. There's a reason for that you know," he said back in a testy voice.

"I've been trying to tell you that everything's so messed up. I just needed to be with you. Can we go somewhere?" I said, trying to rub his chest.

He stepped back. "I'm in a homeless shelter. No guests aloud. Didn't you hear the lady?"

"I found out how my parents really died. It was horrible. I need you."

"Go home, Ansli. Talk to your folks about it. I don't know what you're saying, or I don't understand it all, but right now I'm no good for you."

"But you're my boyfriend."

"Alright, well let me help you out. Let's end that."

"What?" I said in disgust, like I'd just been slapped again.

"You've got to go. I've got to help my mom figure out our lives. Everyone isn't born with a silver spoon."

"Like I was either? Aren't you listening to anything I have to say?"

"Okay, everyone wasn't adopted into a family that can give them a silver spoon. Quit being a brat! Dang! We're through."

Hugo went back inside the place and shut the door in my face. I couldn't believe that when I needed him most, he broke up with me. What audacity!

CHAPTER TWO
ANXIETY

"Okay, so don't ask any questions. Just come and get me!" I said into the receiver to my sister Shelby.

"I'm already in the car driving towards where I think Hugo lives," she said.

"How'd you know I was at Hugo's?"

"'Cause if all that happened to you today happened to me, I wouldn't want to be around my family either. I'd want to be around my man."

Just hearing her say that was comforting. Not because it was true but because she understood me like only a sister could. I texted her the address, and when I saw a McDonald's a few blocks away from the homeless shelter, I told her to meet me there.

I could hardly breathe. It was like a pit from a plum was stuck in my throat or something, and I couldn't get it out. I wasn't choking, but I couldn't ask for help because my body was in trauma. Hugo had dumped me. This was so odd because I agreed to be his girl before I ever physically laid eyes on him. That's just how close we were. Talking to each other, encouraging one another, being there for the other, and now that was gone. I took deep breaths to calm down, but that wasn't helping.

Shelby had been my best friend for years, but Hugo had taken her place. She didn't mind because she was spacey trying to get her clothing designs noticed by the world and blushing everywhere over this Spencer guy, who was actually Mr. Brown's stepson. My sister was living in such a tangled web, but she was working it and weaving it. I hadn't even gotten to tell her my great news that I had a boyfriend because she dropped the bomb first. As soon as I wanted to be all giddy with her, excited with her, and say we could double date or something, I didn't have a man anymore.

Shelby had always been stronger than me, and I admired that so much about her too. I didn't want to cry, but as soon as she pulled up twenty minutes later, I couldn't hold back the tears. She quickly parked the car, got out of it, and gave me the tightest embrace like we hadn't seen each other in years.

"I know this is hard. I know you feel alone, but Mom and Dad are going crazy. Mom was ecstatic when I told her I was on the way to get you."

She just kept talking. I was ready to get in the car and go home, get to my room, close the door, and have none of them say anything to me. However, when I got to the house, my mother rushed outside to Shelby's car, opened the passenger door, and apologized profusely for slapping me, for hurting me, and for breaking me.

"Thank you for coming home, Ansli. I have daughters that I've birthed, but I couldn't love them anymore than I love you. You know that right?" my mom cupped my face with both of her hands and gently said.

It was so funny because it was the exact opposite of how she touched my face hours earlier. Thinking back on the hit, I don't think she was trying to hurt me. She was trying to slap some sense into me. Deep down I knew that it was easy for me to hug her. She was my mom. I didn't want to be emotional though. I didn't want to care, but the tears didn't care what my mind wanted. They were connected to my heart, and they started flowing like rain falls from the sky during a monsoon.

"I can't blame your father. I'm not going to say any of this was his fault. I just didn't want him to keep the truth from you guys. It always felt so wrong, but as the days turned into months, and months turned into years, it just seemed easier for you to continue thinking of your biological dad as a hero because we loved him."

"Mom, please . . . don't." Frustrated, I walked into the house.

My dad was in the family room, and he stood to his feet when I came in. I'd never seen him cry. Big bad Stanley Sharp wasn't crying then, but his eyes were misty.

"You're okay. You're safe," he uttered with relief upon seeing me, but I wasn't smiling. "I know you're angry with me, Ansli, but I was doing what I thought I should. I was trying to protect you."

"Protect me from the truth though, Dad? When you preached to me to always tell the truth? What's the lesson in all this? How could you justify what you did? How was what my father did okay? I don't understand any of it. And worse, I don't understand me."

"What do you mean?" he said in a tone that was a little impatient.

"Letting all this information circle around in my head, it feels like it's going to explode." I said to him as my mom and Shelby came inside. "Where's Yuri? I've got to see my sister."

"She's asleep. She understands," my dad said, suggesting I should hear him out. "Now I need you to as well. We can't prove it, but we think it was the steroids your dad was using. So you understand, he loved your mother, and he loved you girls, and I knew him. No way he would have done this in his right mind. No way."

Processing it all, I shouted, "So then I could just go crazy."

"No, Ansli, don't say that," my mom said as she put her arms on my shoulders.

But I stepped forward so her arms would drop.

My dad said, "See, this is why I didn't want to tell you anything, Ansli, until you're old enough to understand. What happened to him was unfortunate. It's not hereditary. It was the drugs."

"So you admit what my dad did was crazy?"

I don't even know why I said that. Of course it was crazy. The man who brought me into this world killed my mom. Guess I wanted my dad to stop defending him.

"I just need you to grow up in this situation right now. You think I should have told you, then act like you should be able to handle it. Quit going around here making up reasons as to why you should have known when you're acting juvenile, making my point that you shouldn't have known."

"Alright, just calm down, Stanley," my mom said to him.

"I'm frustrated right now. Brown shouldn't have opened his mouth."

"At least he had the balls to tell me the truth," I boldly stated, not caring that my dad wasn't my peer.

At that point, I quickly exited and went to my room. Last thing I wanted was for either of my parents to slap me again, which I probably deserved for being a smart mouth. It had been a heck of a day. I honestly had the right to explode, but I stood there on pins and needles behind my door, hoping that they'd forgive me. Because some lines, just shouldn't be crossed.

***

I didn't know what a heart attack felt like, but if chest palpitations that were becoming more intense by the second were any indication of the onset of a heart attack, then I needed to get to the emergency room. I knew the Sharps loved me, but now there was a distance between us. My belief that the parents that I lost and took comfort in knowing were now angels in heaven looking down on me was now only half true. Surely if my dad killed my mom and himself, he was in hell.

The boyfriend who had my heart broke it. Though it had only been a short time, he meant a lot. I never had a boy take interest in me, care about me, and desire me. People would always comment on how cute I was, but my body was not like Shelby's. She had curves in all the places boys liked. I was just a pretty yellow face, but Hugo thought I was sexy and special. But now, he'd severed ties. How could I calm myself down when my thoughts of my world being shredded like it was paper being destroyed by a paper shredder were making me feel anything but comforted?

When Shelby knocked on my bedroom door and called out to me, I was reminded that I had another problem. The girl I was supposed to love, who was supposed to trust me with her life, now had me envious. I always wanted her parents to really be mine. That was never going to happen. And though they wanted me to believe they loved me the same, I never would. She now had a boyfriend, and I didn't. To make matters worse, she had a dream. She had goals. She had a career, and she was still in high school. She had it going on, and I had nothing.

"Just, just go away, Shelby. Mom and Dad . . . URGH, I can't even believe I keep calling them that. If your parents can leave me alone, then you can too."

"Not okay, I'm about to break down this door, Ansli, if you don't quit pouting and open up! Straight up girl! So we won't both be in trouble. Let me in, please."

Against my better judgment, I let her in, but I didn't want to play nice with her anymore. I didn't want to act like it was all okay. I didn't want her to think I was fine when I wasn't. Yeah, she said she knew I wasn't okay, but the entire ride home she kept on talking. She never really wanted to know what was going on with me. Why should I think she wanted to hear me out now?

"Okay," I said when I opened up the door. "You see I haven't killed myself. Now can you leave?"

"Why are you joking like this?" she said, like she was disgusted with my comment.

"I meant it."

"Please don't talk like that," Shelby said. "I want to make sure you were okay."

I stepped back, and she entered. She put her hands on her head as if she were in pain. Then it dawned on me that, now that we knew about my biological father's final actions of taking his own life, my comment that I didn't commit suicide wasn't funny.

"You see I'm okay. Please get out, Shelby," I said, as my hand touched a water globe on my desk, further upsetting me. The water globe that my dad brought back to all five of us from a trip to England years ago held a princess in her house. I wanted to take it and chuck it at Shelby's face. My world wasn't perfect anymore, and I was angry.

"I don't want to hurt you," I said to her.

"Hurt me? What are you talking about?"

The only thing I could do was tell her the truth. "You have everything."

"We have the same things. My parents are

your parents if that's what you're talking about."

"You know I don't see them that way anymore, so quit pushing that down my throat."

"Okay, what else?"

"Life is just all messed up."

"What are you talking about? With Hugo?" she asked, having intuition that I had to be upset in the romance department. "I don't know everything, Ansli, but I know that like girls have menstrual cycles, guys do go through some type of crisis monthly too, if you ask me."

"What are you saying? Hugo has a period?" I asked her because I didn't know everything there was to know about guys.

I mean, I knew he didn't bleed or anything like that, but still, what was she saying? What did Shelby mean? She was having trouble spitting it out, so I wondered: was she talking smack to be close? Sometimes when we got mad at each other, Shelby would say anything until we laughed and forgot what we were fussing about.

Seeing me squint, she cleared her throat and explained, "No really, I'm saying that they're moody. Just like we are. And while he's tripping today, tomorrow it'll probably be a different story. But you got more going on for yourself than wallowing and being frustrated with stuff going on with a guy."

"No I don't. I don't have anything else going on. You've got your creative brain. You can sit there with a sketchpad and come up with the next greatest design. Instantly, when I see your work, I want to put on your clothes. You've just begun being a designer for real, and you're already going to grand levels."

"Exactly, and I need to take it to another level. I need to brand my stuff. I imagine two S's side by side or crisscross or something, but I don't have skills with all that. I'm talking to Spencer about it because he's great with design, but at the same time, I need to have my work photographed. I need to have myself looking picture perfect. Sydney sent me a list of things that I have to have done. One thing is getting a press kit. She sent me all these photographers' numbers to call. Why should I choose any of them when my sister is the best photographer I know? You're sitting here saying you don't have a talent. You envy me because I'm doing something. Well, we just need to turn what you're good at into a business as well. Because once I see the gorgeous pictures that you're going to create of my clothes and see how good you're going to make me look, because I'm not as beautiful as you, let's just admit it . . . "

"Oh hush," I said, batting my eyes and feeling really appreciative that she saw something special in me too.

She continued, "Everyone's going to want you to take their pictures. So no more whining, no more crying, no more feeling sorry for yourself. I promise you, if you poured your heart and soul into being a full-time photographer then turned that passion into a business, who knows, you may capture images that change the world."

"You really think I could be that great of a photographer?"

"Yeah! Because you always talk junk about how all of us think we're good because we have cell phones, but you're the real deal. So it's time to put up or shut up, Ansli. You were telling me that I could do it. You made me believe in myself not too long ago. And it turned out great. Let's walk down this road together! If I'm going to have a business, you can have one too."

"Just hearing you say that scares me."

"And if it didn't move you at all, then I'd say it wasn't something you should do. But because you feel that you don't want to fail, that's why you're going to succeed." Shelby gave me the biggest hug.

She saw past my flaws and loved me anyway. Shelby gave me hope in her embrace. Though I was nervous about all the big plans she had for me, she was right. Being anxious was a good thing.

***

"There's my boo," Shelby said to me, as she pointed to Spencer who was proudly walking her way. Then she squeezed my hand and started doubting. "What if he's changed his mind about asking me to be his girl and all? What if he doesn't want me?"

"Okay, you are talking so silly. Don't get our lives mixed up," I told her and laughed.

"Look how he's smiling. That guy ain't going nowhere."

"Hey girl!" Spencer said with a glow in his eyes when he looked at Shelby, coming up and giving her a real big hug.

Then he kissed her on the lips, right in front of me. He must not have known she was not into public affection. But maybe I was the one who didn't know my sister because she was not trying to hide that they were together.

"Mhhm, we're in school, not his bedroom," I finally said, making them split apart.

Blushing, Shelby said, "Spencer, I want to introduce you to my sister, Ansli."

"Yeah, we don't have any classes together, so I haven't seen you around," he said to me. "Nice to meet you."

I extended my hand to shake his, but he pulled me to him and gave me a hug too. I was a bit uncomfortable. I mean I didn't know him, and he wasn't my boyfriend. And when Hugo walked by seeing me in the arms of another, I pushed back.

"Okay, you two talk. It was good meeting

you," I uttered and then went to chase my guy. "Hugo!"

But he kept going like I hadn't even called him at all. I was hoping that my sister was right. That whatever was going on with him, in terms of him thinking we didn't need to be together, would pass. But when I saw him walk straight up to the cutest Hispanic girl I'd probably ever seen in my life—look out Jennifer Lopez, for real—I thought my heart was going to break again. He said something in her ear, and the two of them just walked away. What kind of sign was he giving me? Why was he doing me like that? I was actually happy when Slade, Sloan, and Yuri came up behind me. The four of us walked on down the hallway so I didn't have to seem pitiful. I might not have a bunch of friends, but I did have family, even if in my mind that was a big question mark.

At school I wasn't a big socialite. It didn't much matter because, being one of five girls so close in age, we never needed anyone else. Maybe they'd been my crutch. Maybe I was now wanting Hugo to hold me up too. Maybe

I needed to step out of my comfort zone, really take this whole being a professional photographer thing seriously and dig into my strengths. I was so worried about what was upsetting me, trying to make life right, that I wasn't focused on what was already right.

"You're passing our class aren't you?" Sloan said.

I didn't even realize I was already there. I was just coasting down the hallway, contemplating my next steps, not realizing that my next class could change my future. The art room was calling my name. But before I walked in the door, Sloan grabbed my arm.

"I'm sorry," she said as she gave me a hug.

Leery of her gesture, I questioned, "Sorry about what?"

"I was a jerk last night, and I don't want you to think that I'm not angry. I'm mad at our parents too."

"Huh? They didn't do anything to you."

In a serious tone, Sloan said, "If they did something to you, they did something to me. Keeping the truth from you like that, it's like we're living in a house of cards. What else are they hiding that might make our happy home fall down? You know how I feel about the truth."

"Well don't get yourself in trouble because of me."

"I'm just not a fake person. I'm uncomfortable with what they decided, and they need to feel it."

"Thank you, Sloan. Of all people, I never thought you'd be on my side like that."

"I give you a hard time, but you know I love you," Sloan said as she gave me a bump.

Minutes later it was time to get to work. The art assignment actually grabbed my attention. Our teacher, Mr. Lang, who looked like he was probably twelve years old and fresh out of college, encouraged us in our first big project. We had to do a project on capturing pain. If someone could have taken a picture of me yesterday when I found out about my parents, I could have submitted that, and certainly that would have been an A. But it had to be something we either drew ourselves, painted, or took a picture of, and the work had to be titled.

The bell rang, signaling lunchtime. Hugo and I had the same lunch, but I didn't see him anywhere. I was sitting with Slade, and she was babbling on and on about friends.

"You know I'm tired of just hanging with us. I need someone else . . . probably because you and Shelby partner up and Sloan and Yuri partner up. That leaves me by myself anyway. So while it seems like I'm a part of the crew, really I'm not a part of anything."

"What are you talking about, Slade? You sandwich in the middle of us. You're always a part of everything. And the three of you guys are like triplets anyway," I explained alluding to her, Sloan, and Yuri.

As soon as I spotted Hugo across the room, I got up and headed his way. When he saw me, he walked the other way. I was hurt, and folks were staring. I quickly turned back to play it off. My eyes locked on this girl who grabbed some of my food off my tray. Slade was gone and so was my food.

Before I could even say anything she was gone, but I wanted to tell her not to do that again. So I followed her. She was taking stuff off the cafeteria line.

"What are you doing? You're stealing," I caught up to her and said.

"I was just . . . please . . . I'm sorry, okay."

"No, it's not okay."

"You don't know my story."

"You don't know my stomach. And now you're stealing from the cafeteria. It's just not cool."

"Is there some problem going on right here?" Mr. Garner walked up and said.

"No problem. No problem at all," this girl who looked like she clearly needed a bath said to our principal.

"She stole my food! And she just stole from the cafeteria!" I shared, still mad about so much.

Mr. Garner shook his head. "No, Katera. Tell me you didn't."

The Katera chick dashed off.

"Katera!" he yelled out. "I can't let you just do this. We talked about this."

"What do you mean you talked about it? She's done it before?" I said, probably mad at everything else, and saying that just gave me a reason to vent.

"You don't understand, Sharp."

"You know my name?"

"Yeah, of course I do," he said. "You are one of my students with special circumstances."

"Urgh," I uttered hating that. "She's low income. She should be on free and reduced lunch."

"Right, she is."

"So why is she stealing?"

Mr. Garner gave me a real talk. "Because she's homeless. And if I kick her out of here during the day or expel her, not only will she not have any place to go at night, but I'll be taking away the only safe haven she has."

At that point it felt like I had stuck a knife in my own heart. And I hated having all these analogies about killing myself now that I heard my father killed himself, but that was truly how I felt. At first, I wanted the girl gone, and now because I reported it, Mr. Garner had to act on it. Last thing he wanted was for me to be able to tell my dad or anyone else that he wasn't following protocol. If I got her kicked out, there was no way I could live with myself seeing someone wonder the streets.

"So, we have homeless kids at this school?" I mean I knew Hugo's situation, but I guess I just assumed that was an isolated one. He was at least able to stay at a shelter.

Now the principal shook his head. "We've got twenty students at this school who are homeless. I'm trying all I can to help them, but their problems are so massive. It just gives me grave anxiety."

CHAPTER THREE
AWE

"Let me go get Katera. This really can't go on," my principal said. My mouth was already wide open, but that comment practically made it drop to the ground.

"No, no, no, I can't turn her in," I quickly retracted, knowing the horrible fate I would cause this girl.

To think I just thought she was unsanitary. I felt like she should be ashamed of herself because she hadn't taken a bath. Now, I was ashamed of myself because I didn't even realize she couldn't take one. I could only imagine where I'd be if the Sharps hadn't taken me in. Yeah, I knew I had maternal grandparents in Europe somewhere, but they hadn't really reached out to know me and my sister.

My dad was raised by a single mom, and she died before I was born. If not for grace, Kateras's rough situation could be mine.

"Please, please forget I even said anything."

"Ms. Sharp, I'm going to have to report it."

"Report what? What do you think I said?" I questioned, thinking I could recant.

Mr. Garner frowned at me, basically wanting me to know I needed to remember. "That she stole your food."

"No! No, I didn't say that."

"You said she stole food in the cafeteria."

"Nope, didn't see a thing," I said as I winked for him to get that I was changing my mind.

He smiled. "So you're saying . . . "

"Exactly," I said without him even finishing it, then I walked away. "Nothing to report!"

"I will talk to her though!" he shouted out.

Walking to class, I was all screwed up 'cause every person who looked a little untidy, stressed, dirty, wrinkled, smelly, and worse, I wondered if they were one of the twenty homeless kids who didn't have a place to go that was secure from the bugs, the weather, and any other dangers. It really was a thought that I had never comprehended. Sure I was angry at Stanley and Sherri, but when I saw the shelter Hugo, his mom, and his brother were in, I didn't want any part of it. I'd rather be mad at home than have to fight life out there on my own.

I had to find her. I had to apologize. I had to help.

"Hey, it's Katera, right?"

With a stank attitude, she said, "What do you want? I'm probably not even going to be able to come back to school thanks to you."

"It's all good."

"What do you mean it's all good? I heard what you told the principal. I ain't have no mo' chances with him."

"Yeah, when he told me that, I took back what I said."

"He told you?" she said, focusing on the wrong thing. "He's not supposed to tell any student in this school my business."

"No, I mean he told me that . . . "

"Don't try to make up anything."

"Well listen, don't get all smart and uppity when you stole food. I did see it. I did take it back, so what difference does it make what I know? I'm sorry," I said, getting as testy with her as she was getting with me.

"You think I want your help? Thanks, but no thanks."

I had never thought of cutting school, until that moment. The truth remained, Katera needed a bath. While my parents were at work, my sisters had more classes at school, and I had weight training next, which was a class I wasn't interested in because I wasn't an athlete. Since the class was filled with a whole bunch of football players, the coach wasn't going to miss me.

"I owe you this. How about we go to my house? I get you washed up, a meal if you'd like, and we can go from there."

"You're taking me to your house and helping me? No, I don't trust you. Too dang-on good to be true. Ain't nobody trying to help me. Plus I don't have any other clothes to change into."

"We can wash the clothes you have, and I have some you can have."

She stepped closer, looked me up and down and said, "Are you fruity or something?"

"You mean am I gay?" I asked her, a little insulted with how she asked me. "I'm not interested in you if that's what you're asking."

"So you do like girls?"

"What does that matter, Katera? I genuinely want to help. That's all. I'm not trying to be in the bathroom with you. Please trust me when I say I'm not at all attracted to you."

"When I clean up, you will be."

I just gave a quick grin and a short laugh. Then we headed out. She knew which ways to walk out so we didn't get caught. Deep down I knew I was angry to be so reckless and defiant.

As we drove to my house, Katera was fascinated.

"You live on this side of town? Wow, I never even come over here, only heard it was upscale. You got a maid or butler? Not only are you high-yellow, but you're rich too. You've got it made in life."

"What does being high-yellow have to do with anything?" I said, admiring her pretty, dark, mocha skin.

When we got home, I forgot that our house-keeper Senora Romez was there. She started speaking to me in Spanish when I walked through the door. While I couldn't understand everything she was saying, I knew she was asking, "Why are you home so early?" and "Who is this smelling like a stinky cat?"

"We're working on a project," I lied.

I didn't want to get into the habit of lying, skipping school, and just plain old being bad, but I had to tell her something. When I took Katera to my room, she was google-eyed. She picked up the small globe on my dresser and shook it extra hard. I couldn't help but feel like my real world was shaking too.

"This is awesome. Look at all your clothes. This furniture. I saw the picture coming in that you've got a bunch of sisters. How many of y'all share this room?"

"It's mine alone."

"What?"

"Yeah, all of us have our own bedrooms. There're five bedrooms upstairs. I have to share a bath with my sister Shelby, and my three other sisters have to come out in the hallway to share their bath."

"Oooh, that's so bad. They have to come out in the hallway," Katera mimicked. "I don't even know why that's bad."

"I wasn't trying to belittle your situation. I just was explaining mine."

"And I shouldn't be so quick to get angry at all you got."

"Can I ask you a question?" I asked her, and she nodded. "How'd you get like this?"

"It was just me and my mom. She's on drugs somewhere. When I was little, we were staying in this nice house. I thought it was ours, but turned out it was this drug dealer's my mom was working for. When she lost all his money, smoked up all his money, gave away all his money, or whatever she did to all his money, he got pissed. He beat her almost to death. She hasn't really been in her right mind ever since."

"Where is she now?"

"She got locked up."

"Isn't there a Department of Children and Family Services where you can go?"

"I slipped through the cracks, and now that I'm eighteen, there really isn't much they can do for me. So, I don't like stealing, but I gotta do what I gotta do to make it."

She took the towel and soap from my hands, went into the bathroom, and shut the door. And I thought I had problems. Nope, not really. My issues paled in comparison to hers.

***

I was driving with Katera in my car, and I needed to keep my eyes on the road; however, I couldn't keep my eyes off of her. The transformation was amazing! It's crazy what a little soap and water would do. For most folks, a bath makes us better, for her, it made her blossom. Before, her natural locks were so tangled up and dingy looking. Now, they were fresh and cool. I want to run a comb through them, play with them; her hair reminded me of a doll I had when I was little. Most people looked at my straight hair with admiration. I actually wished mine had some resistance.

"What? Haven't you ever seen *Trading Places?*" Katera asked me.

"No, what's that?"

"It's a movie with Eddie Murphy and Dan Aykroyd."

"Okay, what's it about?"

"It's a comedy about two men. One was a bum, and one was a rich guy."

I knew she was insinuating that that was like the two of us. However, I didn't see anything funny in the contrast, nor did I get the correlation as to why I should care. I just looked at her.

Huffing she said, "You're staring at me like I can't clean up, like I couldn't be your equal. If I had all the things you had, well, that's the same thing that happened in the movie. The stupid men who owned everything thinking they could pull strings made a bet that if the rich guy was stripped away from everything, becoming poor would crumble him, and if the poor guy was given much and taught how to be successful, he could be sustained and remain classy."

"They both bet that?"

"No, one thought he could and one thought he couldn't. You should just see the movie because you're making me uncomfortable by looking at me like I'm a freak."

"No, I'm looking at you because you're beautiful."

"Exactly, that's my point. Homeless people can be beautiful if they had the same help everybody else has," Katera schooled.

I didn't know how to respond to that. I was still a kid myself, and so was she. I had lost my parents, and so had she. Why was I on one side of the tracks, and she was on the other? Was it fate? Was it God? Was that just the way it was? I didn't have the answers, and I didn't want to fuss with her. I was getting text messages that I needed to get back home because we had an appointment with my dad for a charity event.

It was now September, and with each day, there was more pressure put on our schedules to accommodate his so we could possibly help him win.

"Where am I taking you?"

"Not some place you would want to stay, but home for me. Turn right here."

We were turning into an abandoned warehouse. I knew she didn't have a true place to live with brick, mortar, a floor, and a ceiling. The place I was pulling up to looked condemned. I kept driving as she insisted, and when we got closer in, even on the outside of the building were little camps, tents, and make-shift structures.

These suspicious guys with gang symbols were hanging out around a couple motorcycles and a beat-up truck. One dude with a patch over his eye spotted Katera. She slouched down. I wouldn't want to cross that crew.

"Hurry, keep going," Katera said, confirming she wasn't comfortable with the guy. "Park here. Come on. I need to introduce you to Momma Dee because she's going to be mad if I don't bring you in to say thank you. We won't be long, and our spot is set up right when we go inside. So you won't have to walk far. No one is going to touch your stuff, but lock your doors."

I reached in my car to get my camera out of the glove department because what I saw was amazing. No words could describe it. Only a picture could adequately tell the story of strength in the midst of suffering. I snapped one man sleeping on a palate like he was lying on the beach with no worries. I saw another lady feeding her two children soup out of a cold can, but the kids were smiling. Then there was an elderly man who had holes in his shoes but who was still walking tall.

Katera snapped, "You really should ask people before you snap their pictures."

"I'm sorry. I'm not going to put it on the Internet or anything. I just . . . I don't know. I followed my instincts, and I really need it for a class project."

"Who is this you have with you?" sweet, plump, Momma Dee said.

"A rich, brat who took pity on me," Katera rudely said.

Momma Dee swatted her arm. "Oh, don't give her a rough time. You look beautiful Katera. I sure wish I had the means to make you look like this every day."

"I don't need to look like this," Katera assured her caretaker when she saw a bit of sadness in Momma Dee's eyes. Then Katera perked up, "But I don't want to get dirty tonight because when I get to school, people are going to be looking!"

The two of them hugged. Momma Dee twirled Katera around. They were so giddy.

I got another text message. I knew I needed to get going. The precious lady couldn't thank me enough. I could tell Katera wanted to as well when her eyes got watery, but she was all tough and only said "bye."

***

About an hour later, I was getting out of the limousine with my family, a steep contrast from the place I'd just been. I was quiet in the car. My parents thought it was because I was still mad at them, which I probably was, but I was also quiet because I couldn't believe what I'd just seen. I was even more shocked when we pulled up to a similar place. We were at a soup kitchen.

Our dad prefaced our community service by saying, "Now I know you guys aren't used to this, but our family's got a chance to serve dinner tonight to some folks having a tough go at it. I expect you to be respectful. We'll be about an hour, and then we'll get going. I know you all have school tomorrow."

I hadn't even looked up in the car, but when we walked in and I saw a lot of the Hispanic people, I realized I was on Hugo's side of town. Just as I thought about him, I saw him at a table giving his food to his little brother. I held Shelby's arm and made my head nod in his direction.

"Go, talk to him. I'll take care of Daddy."

He didn't know what to say when he saw me. I could tell he wanted to smile, but it also looked like he wanted to cry.

"I'm sorry for interrupting your dinner. I'm not following you. My family, we're . . . "

"What? Volunteering here tonight? I didn't even know you were here. I got you." He stood and shocked me when he said, "I've been over the top mean to you, and I've been wrong. The one good thing that was going on in my life was you. You helped me see that my doodling is art and uh, if we can be close friends again . . . "

I leapt in his arms and hugged him so tight. I probably shocked everyone in there, but it didn't matter to me. A guy who had nothing and a girl who had everything, in the eyes of the world, were not really equal. However, to me we were equal because everything to me was him, and he finally realized he was nothing without me.

***

"Oooh, alright now. Step back! You're hugging my baby a little too close. Ansli, give me an introduction. Who is this young man?" my dad embarrassed me by saying.

Reluctantly, I said, "Dad this is Hugo."

"And Hugo is?"

I didn't know whether I could say he was my boyfriend. I thought Hugo was saying we could get back together, but I was trying not to be embarrassed in front of my dad, and I wasn't even sure if it was a good idea to tell my dad I had a boyfriend.

Rolling my eyes, I said, "A friend."

"If I may, sir?" Hugo said, surprising me by talking in such a polite tone. "I'm Hugo Green, and Ansli and I are really good friends."

I held my head down at that moment. Really good friends is not what I wanted him to say. But whatever.

"I don't know if I buy 'really good friends' from that hug," my dad said in a cool tone.

"Alright, well I know y'all are busy, sir, so I'm not going to keep you talking to me," Hugo said, starting to walk away.

My dad touched his shoulder, "No, no, no. Anyone who's a friend of my daughter and has got her interest, which I can see by her eyes you've got her interest, I'm interested in."

"Well, I just don't think I'm worthy to be her friend. I mean you're meeting me at a soup kitchen. How do I look asking you if I can talk to your daughter?"

"It's not where you are that impresses a father, son. It's where you plan to go. How high you're aiming? What kind of heart you have? What you do with your time . . . giving your little brother your food is honorable. I understand you're only able to get a certain amount here so that they can feed everybody."

I hadn't even realized my dad saw that. I saw that too, but to know he did and was impressed made me feel good. Hugo was a good person, even if I wanted to kick him in the shin for not saying he was my boyfriend. I could see my father was helping to give him pride. His mother came over and talked to my father about her struggles, and he said he wanted to help her.

Hugo's mom said, "I knew you were a good man. There's something I want to show you. Hugo, give me your drawing pad."

"No, no . . . I'm embarrassed. No."

"What's on the drawing pad?" my father asked.

I was wondering the same thing. When Hugo's little brother handed his mom the tablet, there were so many drawings that were out of this world. Then she flipped to a page where it had, "Stanley Sharp, Mayor of Charlotte," and it wasn't in my father's current logo for running for mayor, but it was one he would be able to use if he won.

"See, my son believes in you. When you win, you could license this. 'License,' that's the right word, Hugo, right?" his mom asked with bright eyes and big hopes.

"He's not interested in that, Mom. They've got professional people for that."

"Well, I can't imagine anyone creating anything better. Most things are digital, but some of the greatest designs come for sketches. You're talented. Can I have this? I don't want to be presumptions that I'm going to win, but right now, I'd love to buy it from you. Is two-fifty good?"

His mom was so excited. Hugo didn't know what to say. I was thankful too. My dad wrote his mom a check. It was time for us to go after my dad met more people.

My dad stepped over the door and said, "Can I have your attention?"

There were about seventy people in the room, and I loved that there were no cameras. My dad began.

"I'm Sterling Sharp. This is my wife Sherri and our daughters. Many of you may know, but if you don't, I'm a candidate running for mayor of this great city of Charlotte. Last time I checked, anyone who was a citizen of our great city had the opportunity to go out and vote, so I'm hoping you guys do. I'm here today because I wanted to show you that I care about who you are and what you're going through. Life is tough and can knock us down sometimes, but as your mayor, I'll understand that we need to help each other rise above our challenges. I'm going to put together a task force that can help people transition out of poverty. So over the next couple of weeks, I'll be coming back. Not only to serve food, but to listen to things you think your city government can do to help. When we get all of our citizens on their feet, the taller Charlotte can stand. So, you stay encouraged. I'm a man of faith, and I believe we can handle a rough night, but joy comes in the morning. You might be going through your season, and you might not feel good where you are, but that's alright. We're going to put a plan together to get you back to work. Stay Sharp."

People stood to their feet and clapped for him. Hugo was among them, and that made me feel good. It was good that my father was giving people with no hope something to hope for, but it wasn't good when I got in the car and all of my family wanted to know what was going on with me and Hugo.

***

I actually couldn't wait to see Hugo the next morning when I walked into Marks High School. I hoped he would say we were boyfriend and girlfriend again, but I couldn't find him. Instead, the principal walked up to me.

"I'm having a meeting with the homeless kids in our school during second period, and because of what happened earlier in the week, I just felt like maybe you would want to be there and encourage them."

"Yes, sir. Count me in."

"Alright, I'll get you a pass out of class. I know you'll be able to share something encouraging."

When I was standing before about fifteen of the twenty homeless kids, I was a little uneasy because they were looking at me like, "you're not homeless; why are you here?" They were sizing me up like most kids do them, thinking I was cocky, had a hard heart, and didn't really care. I wasn't trying to look down on them, and I wanted them to know it. If only Hugo and Katera were in there to vouch for who I was, it wouldn't be so hard, but they weren't, and I couldn't worry about that now because there were people in front of me whom I needed to connect with.

"I don't even know why you're in here, rich girl," said this guy who sported a necklace with the name Freddie on it.

"Yeah, why should we listen to anything you have to say?" one girl said.

"Because it's not fair that other people look away like your problems don't matter, and I can't speak for other people, but your problems matter to me. I know how it is to go through stuff. I've been living for the past fourteen years without my biological parents. I was told that they were killed when I was three, but that's not even true. I just learned that my dad killed my mom and then killed himself. If it wasn't for a family who took me and my little sister in, who knows where I'd be. So, I'm not standing before you because I'm perfect. I'm standing before you because I'm just as broken. If you can look at me and see someone who you think has it together, then you can be just like me, if not better. We've just got to help each other and figure it out.

"No one should be homeless, be hungry, and have to deal with adult problems at our age. I don't know a lot of people, but I know some people who can help. They just need to know. So, I need you guys to tell me what's going on so we can try to fix some of this stuff. I care. Until we get you all some better situations, I'm not going anywhere."

It was like the people I was talking to changed. They sat up straight, and their eyes got brighter. I saw some smiles and grins, and the frowns went away. They were looking at me like they believed what I was saying finally. I was happy that they did because I was real.

Freddie said, "I just can't believe you told us your real business. Your dad killed your mom and himself? Dang, that's deep. Maybe you are being straight up with us. We do need some help. I'm not just believing you care like that for real, for real. I'm in awe."

CHAPTER FOUR
ATTITUDE

"What is wrong with you, Hugo?" I said as soon as my guy got into my car at the same McDonald's Shelby picked me up from days earlier.

"Did you have to tell your sister and her boyfriend to follow you? He's driving his girl around, but you have to come pick me up," Hugo uttered, clearly with a bruised ego.

"We are all going to the football game, and we had to pass this way. Actually, I can leave my car here, and we can get in the car with them. Let's all go together."

"What? You just don't want to drive or

something?" He looked at me awkwardly and said. "I want to spend time with you. I don't want to be uncomfortable."

"Well, I don't really know Spencer either."

"So, why are you trying to force us to hang? Are you able to drive? Do you have gas?"

"Yeah, I'm straight with all that," I said as he threw his hands in the air like "okay then." "Okay, well let me just tell my sister."

I turned off my car, got out, and headed over to the other car. My sister was motioning for me to hurry. Opening the backdoor, Spencer had gotten out thinking I was going to get in the backseat of his car.

Quickly, I said, "No, no, no, that's okay. I just came to talk to Shelby."

"Y'all not going to ride with us?" he asked, squinting like that made no sense.

In my mind I was thinking, 'I just said I wanted to talk to my sister about this,' but since he was pushing me, there was no need to be rude, so I said, "Yeah, I'm going to drive."

"No, you can't drive. It's far. It's farther than Concord, up I-85," Shelby yelled out.

Shelby was trying to convince Hugo that we should all ride together, but I dashed around to the front and blocked her from going to him.

"No, leave it alone."

"Well, what is his problem? He'd rather you drive a long way than be in the car with us and have a guy drive? I mean shucks!"

"This isn't the old days. I'm perfectly capable of driving, and you and your guy need time to talk like we do."

"I just don't want you to be alone with a nutcase," she said to me.

Rolling my eyes, I said, "Shelby."

"I'm not judging. I'm just saying. If he's going through and making you feel all bad, then maybe you shouldn't be alone with him."

I kept Shelby from going over to talk to Hugo. However, I didn't see that Spencer went over there and tried to convince him. Obviously, it didn't work. Spencer came back to his car and said, "Don't worry about it, Shelby. Just let them follow us."

My sister huffed. When I turned, I could tell Hugo was mad. Before I walked away, my sister grabbed my arm.

Shelby whispered, "You get behind us. Make sure you keep up, but if anything happens or if you need me, call me. You can't text because you'll be driving. Flash us, and we'll pull right over."

I shook my head. I wasn't mad, simply irritated. I knew she cared, but I could take care of myself.

As soon as I got to the car, Hugo looked like I annoyed him. "What did you say to them? Why did you tell them I didn't want to ride with them?"

"I didn't," I told him.

"Yeah, but you told them something to come over and sweat me . . . trying to change my mind."

"Whatever Hugo. Believe what you want. We're driving on our own. What they think doesn't matter. Dang," I said, truly frustrated.

Hugo looked out the window as we pulled out of the parking lot and didn't say two words to me. As we drove in silence, I tried to lead the conversation. "How is your mom?" "How is your brother?" "How are things coming?"

"How are you feeling?" I wanted to say, "How about you quit being a jerk and talk to your girl?" but I didn't. I was too afraid that he would bail on me. What kind of relationship was that?

So I finally said, "You know what? If we're going to be together, we need to be able to communicate. You can't just act like I'm bothering you. You're the one who wanted the two of us to drive alone. If you weren't going to say anything, we could've been in the car with my sister and her boyfriend, at least I could've been talking to them."

Grunting, Hugo said, "What do you want me to say?"

"I want you to open up and tell me the truth. Why are you so hot under the collar?"

"Because I can't take care of you like he can. You think I like it that you had to come pick me up at a McDonald's? You think I'm excited that I don't have any cologne I could put on so I could smell good and look good for my girl on our date? You think as a man I'm alright that I don't have two nickels to rub together, especially when I'm double dating with this dude who seems like he's rolling in dough?"

"Do you think I want to be with you because of the material things you can give me?" I asked, needing him to know that was not the answer. "My dad already gives me enough. We connected online before we ever met, held hands, or kissed. We have a deep relationship, a strong bond, and a connection that is serious."

"I don't know. When your dad gave me that check for the design I made, you seemed happy."

"Yeah, because you got skills and deserve to be paid for that."

"I deserve for your poppy to give me pity money? I don't think so."

Insulted, I frowned. "It wasn't pity money."

"And the sad thing is though my pride wanted to give it back, I couldn't because we needed it so desperately. I'm just tired of being poor."

"Most people in life are tired of something. My dad always says, 'Everybody has issues, but successful people are the ones who can manage their issues well'."

"How do you manage living in a homeless shelter?"

I put my right hand on his hand and said, "I can only imagine that's hard, but you don't take it out on your girlfriend."

When I socked him lightly in the jaw, he said, "Point taken."

***

Our team won the football game, and it was actually good sitting in the stands with Spencer and Shelby. Hugo liked him. When let his guard down, they actually got along pretty well.

The good times ended when, after the game, Spencer said, "Let's go to Red Lobster to eat. We passed one on the way in."

Immediately, Hugo got tense. "Nah, I can't afford that man."

"I got you. I got you guys," Spencer smiled and said.

Hugo got angry and said, "No, I don't need you to have us. You and Shelby, if you guys want to go on to Red Lobster, Blue Lobster, or Brown Lobster, y'all do that, but me and Ansli, we ain't rollin' like that."

"Why you gotta be all uptight about it,

man?" Spencer stepped to Hugo and flexed.

"I ain't uptight. I just don't want a handout. Come on Ansli, let's go," Hugo retorted.

In a softer voice Spencer said, "Dang, man. You don't have to get upset about it. Sorry. We're a long way from home."

"I know how to read the signs. We can get back just fine," Hugo said.

Hugo took my hand and pulled me toward the parking lot. I knew he was embarrassed. I knew he wished he had more. I knew he felt belittled, but no one was trying to make him feel that way, and he didn't have to have an attitude.

***

"I just can't believe you, Hugo. It's gonna be all weird everytime we get together," I said when we got to my car of the stadium parking lot as I jerked away from him, totally angry. "Maybe you had the right idea when you broke up with me. Though I didn't like it then and I wanted you back so much, this ain't working."

He just stood there looking at me, like he couldn't believe I was saying what I was saying.

But I meant it. It really didn't matter what he thought about it. He'd ticked me off.

"Get in!" I shouted after unlocking the door and getting in myself.

He got inside, but wouldn't let me start the car. He put his left hand on my right hand, which was on the ignition. I looked at him a bit disgusted.

Hugo sweetly uttered, "Come on. We should be able to talk about this, Ansli. I'm sorry. I was rude. I'm sorry if it seems like I'm a jerk. I care about you. You know I do. I want to be able to pay when I'm out with you. I just didn't want someone else to feel like he had to take care of what's my responsibility to handle."

"My problem with it, Hugo, is that you thought he was taking pity on you. You didn't have to get defensive. All he wanted to do was have a good time at a very nice restaurant and make sure you had no worries about it. Who knows? The way life is tomorrow you might be helping him out."

"How am I going to help him out when I live in a homeless shelter, Ansli? You're talking crazy."

"No I'm not. He could fall down, and you could have to pick him up. He could need help with a homework assignment, and you could tutor him. He could need a friend, and you could be there. Everything isn't about dollars and cents," I explained.

"When you have no money, everything is about dollars and cents, okay? It's the haves and the have-nots. My mom says it all the time. I see how we're treated. Not because I'm Hispanic, not because I'm a male. People look at me like I'm going to steal their purses sometimes . . . "

I looked at him like 'really?' and he nodded. "Yeah, that junk don't just happen to black guys. Black and white folks think Hispanics want to steal from them too, and it all stems from the fact that most of us are poor."

"Y'all are just frugal, living two and three families in one place . . . supporting each others' businesses. My dad talks about it all the time. If other races follow the strength you guys have, we'd be a better nation."

"You don't understand. You don't know what it's like to walk in my shoes. You don't know what it's like to not be able to help your mom stay in her house."

"That's not your responsibility," I shouted, knowing he wasn't his mom's husband.

"In my culture, if I need to get a job and drop out of school, that's what's expected of me. My mom doesn't want me to do that, but I've already gotten the message from my relatives who don't live in the United States that dropping out is what I need to do. So, forgive me if I'm stressed out and don't want to take a hand out."

My phone rang and, although it was my mom, I was actually happy to answer it to break some of the tension building in my car. "Hey, Mom."

"Hey. Is the game over?"

"Yes, ma'am."

"Okay, well you and Shelby be careful please."

"Yes, ma'am we will."

"We probably won't be home 'til three in the morning."

"How did the fundraising event and rally go?"

"It was great. I missed you and Shelby with us, but your sisters did good for Dad. Slade even sung," my mother shared.

"No way. Dad let her?"

"Yup. I know you girls will be asleep when we get in, so make sure you lock the doors and set the alarm. It worries me that the guard gate isn't up in the front of the neighborhood."

"Alright, Mom. Are you guys on your way back now?"

"No, we're going to finish up at this last reception. Dad thought it would be rude if we cut out early. Your sisters are upstairs in the hotel room."

"Well, you guys should just stay."

"No, we're going to get back to you and Shelby."

"Mom, we're fine. You guys should stay. We're seniors."

"We might, we might. Call me when you get home. Where's your sister?"

"She's not right here right this second," I said, knowing my folks thought we were together.

"Then where is she?"

"Not far away. I can tell her to call you right back," I lied.

"Alright. Y'all just stay together."

"Yes, ma'am."

Quickly, I dialed my sister.

"Hey, you okay?" Shelby immediately said, always caring about me.

"Yeah."

"Well, Spencer's sorry if he offended Hugo."

"Don't worry about all that."

"We're going to stop off and get something to eat."

"Good, but I called 'cuz Mom is trying to get you, so you need to call her back. Heads up they're not coming back until three though."

"Ooh yes, that's good," Shelby said. "Spencer and I are just going to hang out. We're going to the restaurant up here. Can you get back alright?"

"No problem."

"Alright, I'll be home in about a couple hours."

"Before, three o'clock though. You better be good," I told my sister.

"Or good at trying," she said in a slick kind of way.

I didn't know what that meant, but I hung up the phone. Was Shelby ready to get busy? Thinking about that possibility for her, I was nervous and excited at the same time.

"I think I know the way back," I mumbled to myself.

"Just keep straight. The interstate is going to be up here on your left," Hugo replied.

"Oh, okay."

I was really irritated. I didn't know what to say to him. As we neared the city limits of Charlotte, he started talking to me. He got extra touchy feely as he took his hand and stroked my hair. The way he was staring I could tell he was now enticed.

"I'm sorry. I care about you. I think about you at night. I got a lot going on, and I don't want to go back to the shelter right now. Let's be together. One of the things that helps me sleep at night is that I see you in my dreams. Can they become a reality tonight?" Hugo voiced in a husky tone, as he leaned in and kissed my neck.

"Stop," I said, not even realizing that I got off on the exit near my house. However, since I did, and since my folks weren't home, and since he was making me feel all hot with his touches, I said, "I'm taking you to my house."

"Really?" he said, as his hand started sliding between my legs.

I removed his hand, got out of the car, and said, "I want to show you some of my pictures and get your take on them."

He got out and nodded. As we walked to my door, he seemed a bit distant again. I felt like he was pulling away because my house was like a mansion.

Needing to make sure he didn't get bummed out, I said, "Now, though my parents and sisters aren't home, I'm not taking you here so you could feel like, 'Oh, I live in this great big place and you . . . '"

But before I could even say any of that, he moved my head to the back of the door and kissed me passionately. Our hands were roaming all over each other. I guess I was still sort of mad at him, but I was crazy about him at the same time. We made it inside, and one thing lead to another. I didn't show him my pictures. I showed him something more intriguing—my bare body. And he liked what he saw.

**

His kisses on my neck made me feel like I was floating in outer space. I wanted him to send me to the moon. I wanted to lose my virginity with him, but I had to be safe.

As hard as it was to pull away, I said, "Where's the protection?"

"I don't have any, baby," he said as he came back and started licking in my ear.

I never breathed so deep and hard in my life. The passion was exhilarating, and it was so easy for me to surrender and let him have his way. But my brain just shouted, "No!"

"I can't without protection," I uttered.

"When was your last cycle?"

"Huh?" I said, not wanting to discuss any of my personal business like that with him, but, reluctantly, I did. "Last week."

"Then you're fine."

Confused, I said, "How do you know?"

"My mom schooled me on all this. A time that a girl can get pregnant is during the middle of her cycle."

"Well, if mine was last week, I'm close to the middle. Uh uh, stop! No."

I reached down, grabbed my clothes, and dashed to the bathroom. Quickly, I splashed water on my face. I was trippin' anyway thinking of going all the way in my parent's home. Though, they might be spending the night away, they could also be pulling up in any moment. When the doorbell went off, I had a panic attack.

"Oh my gosh! I'm going to get in so much trouble. Where is my bra? Where are my panties? Oh my gosh!"

I was even more scared when Hugo started banging on the bathroom door. "Somebody's here."

"I'm going to be in so much trouble," I said to him as I threw on my clothes, pants inside out, shirt on backwards, and took no time to put on underwear.

"It's got to be Shelby," Hugo said. "She rode with Spencer, so he's got to be dropping her off. Your parents wouldn't be ringing your door-bell."

"When they're in the limousine, they forget their key sometimes, and I haven't even checked my phone to see if they called to say they were on their way. It could be them!"

"Just stay behind me. I don't want you going near the door by yourself," he said. "What if it's not your parents."

"Then we have nothing to worry about."

"It could be someone trying to rob you guys."

"Not in my neighborhood."

"You must not have been watching the news lately."

Forgetting what he was saying, I went to go open the door. Who was this, I wondered? I was startled to find Katera standing before me shaking like she'd been left out in a blizzard for days.

"Come in," I quickly said to her.

When she stepped inside, I looked outside and saw a car driving away.

"How'd you get here?"

"I got dropped off."

When she looked up at me, I saw a black eye.

"What in the world is going on?"

"It's a long story. It's definitely not what you think. I got kicked in the eye, and it wasn't on purpose."

"That doesn't even sound right. Come on. You need a blanket, and a bath, and a bed."

Hugo stepped into view and said, "You need to get me home before your parents get back."

"I didn't know you had company. I had no other place to go," Katera voiced as she held her head down.

I leaned in and asked, "I thought you were staying at that place."

"No, Momma Dee and me had to bounce," Katera said, as I squinted. "Remember the guys who were on motorcycles?"

"Yeah, I remember from when I took you back that time," I said as I shivered thinking of the thugs.

"They just make it difficult for everyone staying back there."

"Did they do this to your face?" I said as I looked at the deep black and blue bruise. She quickly looked away. "Okay, well come on and go with me in the car. I gotta get Hugo home."

"I don't know. I'm too tired. I just need to take a quick bath, please."

Hugo's eyes were saying to me "there is no way you can leave her here." Then I got to thinking that if my parents came back, checked in on me, and saw she was in my bed, they wouldn't come over to give me a kiss and all that good stuff. Even my sister wouldn't bother me if I was sleep. I always had to ask my parents' permission for anyone to stay over. Out of the five of us girls, I never had anyone stay over, so I'm sure when I explained everything, all would be okay.

Just sticking with my gut, I said, "Okay, take a bath. You know where my room is. Just get in the bed and shut the door. I'll be right back."

"No rush," Katera said, being kind. "When are your parents coming back?"

"I don't think they're coming back until the morning . . . "

Hugo was coughing like I was giving her way too much information, but he didn't know Katera. I was a little salty with him anyway. He wanted to put his hand in the vanilla pudding, but he didn't have a glove. He and I thought differently. Though he was my first boyfriend, I didn't want to set a precedent for myself of letting a man run over me.

***

"Smile!" I said when I grabbed my phone and snapped a picture of her.

"Why'd you do that?" she asked insulted.

"Your eye looks bad. Always have evidence," I said to her. "This is in case you report it."

"I told you it was an accident. Please erase it, and don't post it anywhere," Katera angrily barked like a pit bull.

"I'm not going to erase it. I'm not going to post it either. Calm down," I said, before leaving out.

All the way to the shelter Hugo was giving me grief. "You don't know her. You should've made her come with us. You didn't even tell

Shelby she was there. What if she scares your sister? What if your parents come home and they do go in your room to check on you? Why are you putting yourself out there for this girl?"

Finally, I got tired of him drilling me and said, "You of all people said people going through need help, not handouts all the time. I'm trying to help."

"Yeah, but you don't need to be stupid with the help either. It just didn't seem right, and who was flying out of your neighborhood all crazy?"

He went on to explain that when I opened the door, a car sped away. He was paranoid. When we pulled up to the shelter, I leaned over and gave him a kiss.

Changing the subject, I playfully jabbed him, "Next time be prepared."

"I got this prepaid phone. Please, call me when you get home so I know everything is okay," he said, changing the subject back to my safety.

"Alright. Alright."

When I got back to my house, it looked like Grand Central Station outside. I hadn't been gone for an hour, but there were police, there were my parents, there was Shelby, and they all were looking at me. Had something happen to Katera? I ran inside the house, and I was at a loss for words when I saw that our great room was ransacked. Flat-screen television, gone. Computer at the workstation, gone. The speakers from the surround sound, gone. And who knew whatever else was missing?

"Where is Katera?"

I ran upstairs and saw my bedroom empty, but there was a note on my bed that said, "Sorry." Was Hugo right? Did she trick me? Did she take advantage of me? I could not believe she stole from my family after I helped her. At that moment, I was gritting my teeth while tears were pouring down my face. I wasn't sad. I was angry. And honestly if I saw her again, I'd punch her in her other eye, beat that heifer, and kick her tail. I showed her kindness, and in return she stole from me? I was heated and had a boiling attitude.

CHAPTER FIVE
ALIKE

Both my mom and my dad rushed up to me with a look of pure disappointment on both of their faces. Out of five girls, I'd never been the bad one. I wasn't brash like Shelby, bold like Slade, but I wasn't brazen like Sloan either. Nobody was as sweet as Yuri, who barely said a peep, but I didn't give my folks any problems. Now that wasn't the case anymore.

"I'm sorry," I looked at both of them and said, throwing my hands up in the air and trying to control the emotions that were stirring up inside of me.

"You're going to have to give us more than that, Ansli," my dad said.

"Go easy, Stanley," my mom said to him.

I didn't deserve any mercy. I didn't deserve for them to be sweet to me. I didn't deserve for them to cut me slack. They deserved the truth. I'd been angry at them for not being honest with me for so many years. I'd be a hypocrite if I did anything other than that. I had to stand up, take a deep breath, put both of my shoulders back, look them both in the eye, and tell them the truth, but when I tried that, the words just wouldn't come out.

So I repeated, "I'm sorry."

I dashed away from them only to run straight into my four sisters. We were a close family, but at this time, I wanted to be alone. It was my fault our house was no longer a safe haven. It was a mess, and I had to face the music. I sank to the floor and sobbed when they wouldn't move.

"I knew Mom and Dad shouldn't have left you and Shelby alone. What? Did your little broke boyfriend do this?" Sloan uttered, making me look back at her.

It wasn't how she said what she said. She should be angry. I messed up. And it wasn't that she had the audacity to say what she said to me. She should be mad. I messed up. It wasn't that she got her facts totally right. I mean, I messed up. She needed to say what she thought. The problem was that if she had all facts right, she wouldn't go around accusing the wrong person.

"Why do you think it's him?" Shelby asked her, knowing that's what I was wondering.

Sloan rolled her eyes and Slade piped in, "We remember seeing them all cozy at the food kitchen we volunteered at."

"It's not impossible. Desperate people do crazy stuff," Sloan added.

Sloan was angry. Slade and Shelby looked concerned. Yuri knelt down and put her arm around me. I knew she felt my pain.

"Girls, we need to talk to your sister," my mom came in the room and said.

"It's going to be okay," Yuri said as she hugged me.

Shelby extended her arm and pulled me up. "I can stay if you want me to."

"Shelby, did you hear your mom?" my dad said, giving her no choice.

"Just say the word, and I can stay if you want me to," she whispered.

"No, I'm fine. Well, I'm not fine, but I gotta deal with this."

Shelby was about to leave, but my dad said, "Wait a minute, you know what, hold up. See, I thought the two of you guys were supposed to be together. What happened?"

"It was my fault, Dad," I said.

I didn't want to go into all the details, so I knew I needed to hurry up and get to the point, or I was going to make it a lot worse.

"And don't you leave out anything, Ansli," my mother said, giving me that lawyer eye.

She was an interrogator. That's what she did for a living. Almost a human lie detector test. So, for the next twenty minutes, instead of worrying about my consequences, I shared everything.

"So not only did you let a boy in here we never gave you permission to hang out with in the first place, but you befriended a girl who was homeless, and you let her stay here while you took him back to the homeless shelter?" my dad repeated for clarity.

"I didn't think that she would steal anything."

My mom disappointingly said, "Of course you didn't. You didn't think at all."

Still confused, I said, "But I wasn't gone that long. And I knew Shelby was on her way back."

"You know what, just go to bed. I can't even deal with you right now," my mom demanded.

My parents said I couldn't drive the car. My dad started taking off his belt like he wanted to spank me. Of course he didn't, but they were pissed. I couldn't get in my room fast enough, but Shelby had to come through the bathroom that we shared.

"I don't need you to grill me. I know it was stupid," I told her, holding out my arm.

Shelby came closer, "I'm just glad you're okay because whoever helped her take stuff from our house could've hit you in the head and still done the same thing."

"Even if you were here?"

"Yep, they could've beat both of us. Though, I wouldn't have let her tail come in here trying to make people have pity on her."

"Hugo told me. I can't believe she had help to steal from me? Wait until I see her." Processing what Shelby was saying, I went from being angry to being grateful. I hugged my sister so tight. "If anything would have happened to you . . . I'm already feeling terrible that the house is trashed, but you, Shelby. Oh my gosh! And they know where we live. They might come back."

"Don't worry. The police are all over this, but if you have any idea who did this, you need to tell."

I so hoped that Hugo would pick up the phone. I knew he said it was prepaid, and he wanted me call when I got home. On the first ring when he answered, "Hello?" I just started crying.

"What's wrong? Did you get into an accident?" he asked.

"No! Katera stole from me. When I got home, my house was wrecked. It's a mess Hugo, and I think I know who did it."

I went on to tell him that when I dropped her off before, I saw suspect looking thugs. That day Katera explained to me that they were a gang hanging out near homeless people, taking advantage of them, threatening them, and making them take advantage of citizens.

"You can't just tell your dad. You've got to have some proof. They need to be picked up and locked up so they can't hurt anybody.

"My dad knows all kinds of people. I mean, he is running for mayor."

"You don't want to awaken the undertaker do you?"

"What do you mean?"

"You figure it out."

"They could kill him?"

"With bad people, you want to be sure you accuse the right folks. When people are down on their luck, they'll do anything. Murder wouldn't be out of the question, that's all I'm saying."

Boy, was he scaring me, but I knew there had to be a way to help people in need so that they wouldn't do desperate things. I was determined to turn this horrible thing into something positive. Katera and her crew needed help more than ever. Jail wouldn't hurt either.

***

Somehow after cleaning up, meeting with investigators, talking to insurance adjustors, picking out new items to replace what was taken, and being grilled over and over and over again by my parents, I made it through the weekend. I hated that I lost my car privileges for a while. My sister Slade was excited. She had gotten her license, and my parents hadn't bought her a car yet. Now she was able to drive mine. I wasn't mad at her; it was my own fault. Still, it seemed weird being driven to school by my younger sister. Shelby told me I could've ridden with her, but she had to go in early, and I wasn't trying to do that.

Now I was at school. The first person I had to find was Hugo, and like a great boyfriend, he was waiting for me in the parking lot, which was more than I could've hoped for. We didn't have to waste a second. And not caring that my younger sisters were looking, I leapt right into his arms.

"Are you going to introduce us or what? I remember we saw him last time, but he only met Dad," Sloan called out.

"He knows Shelby," I said.

"No I feel like I know all you guys," he said. "Slade is driving now, and she's got the beautiful face and voice."

"Oh wow, stop it," Slade said.

Hugo continued, "Yuri, you look just like Ansli. I could kiss you, thinking you're my girl-friend."

"Watch it now. I'm not your girlfriend," Yuri said as she stepped back.

"He's joking," I said to my little sister.

"I know, I'm just telling him I'm not you. Even, though he is kind of cute," Yuri laughed and said to the side.

"So who am I?" Sloan curled up her lips.

"I don't know. Uhm . . . "

"You didn't tell him anything about me?" Sloan said with her hand on her hip.

"Trust me. I did," I said to Sloan.

"I'm just kidding. You're Sloan. The one she admires for being able to articulate her thoughts like none other."

"Really? You said that about me, Ansli? Thanks girl!" Sloan said.

"Look, y'all have to excuse us," Hugo said, taking my arm.

"Yeah, we have to get going," I winked and said to the three of my siblings as they followed us in.

Hugo and I were both thinking alike, as we both squeezed each other's hands really tight. We didn't have much time before school was going to begin, and Dr. Garner, our principal, was already guarding the front door. Usually he was anywhere but on bus duty. Why this morning of all mornings was he on the look out?

"Sharp girls! Come here," he waved us over.

I let go of Hugo's hand.

"What? You're embarrassed about me or something?" Hugo asked in a salty voice.

"This man knows my dad. I'm already in trouble. Don't take it personal," I said, not wanting to argue with him, but needing him to chill.

"You all okay? I heard there was a big incident at your house this weekend," Principal Garner inquired.

Was there anything this man didn't know about what went on with our family? Sure I got that people were trying to brown-nose because it looked like my dad was going to win the election, but nothing was a sure thing. Yeah, he was running against two idiotic opponents who, in my opinion, paled in comparison, but voters still had to turnout. Maybe this is what folks did to ensure their alliances and make sure they were in good standing just in case their candidate won.

"Yes, sir. There's nothing to report," Sloan said just as irritated as I was at the question.

She waved her little finger in the air, and as if they were her entourage, Slade and Yuri followed her into the school.

"Hold up, Ansli. Is this guy bothering you?" Dr. Garner said, referring to Hugo.

"Why did you ask if I was bothering her?" Hugo asked, completely offended.

I put my hand on his chest. "No, sir. This is my boyfriend, Hugo."

"Your boyfriend? Your dad knows about this?" Dr. Garner questioned.

Getting upset Hugo said, "Sir, why is that any of your business if her father knows?"

"I'm not talking to you right now," Dr. Garner snapped.

Trying to calm the situation, I said, "He and my father are friends so . . ."

"So, that gives him the right to ask personal questions?" Hugo said under his breath. "He's the principal, but he's not your dad."

I opened my eyes real wide. I hoped Mr. Garner hadn't heard my boo. Though Hugo had a point, was this something worth fighting?

"You wait right there." The principal stepped to the side and motioned for me to follow him. "I know you've been spending time with some of our students who are less fortunate, but I didn't mean for you to take that to the extreme. Some students aren't necessarily the best match, you know, boyfriend material. In this day and age, I need to be careful of what I say, but you're right. As your dad's friend, the fact that he trusts you guys to come to my school when there are others in the city he could've had you girls attend, I'm protective. And because you got close to Katera, I believe she was the one responsible for ransacking your house."

"So you do know all the details."

"Your dad and I talk. I mean, he's concerned. I know from Katera's file that this is possible."

"Have you seen her here today?"

"No I haven't, but the police were called. They do plan on questioning her. You need to be careful with the company you keep."

"Principal Garner, one of the candidates for the murals," a secretary from the office came over the walkie-talkie and said to our principal, "is in the office waiting for you, sir."

"Murals? What murals are we getting?" I asked as a thought was coming to my mind.

"We're getting some in the gym, in the cafeteria, and in the front hallway. So, we're interviewing several artists. It's going to be pretty nice."

"How would one go about being considered?" I asked.

"Oh, you paint now?"

"No, but he does," I said, pointing at Hugo.

"Absolutely not. I'm not dealing with a hot-head with something this important. This isn't chicken-scratch I'm expecting to see on these walls. We're paying good money."

"And shouldn't a student have the right to apply? I mean isn't that fair? Don't you think all of the board members and great citizens of this school district would appreciate the principal at least considering a student before dismissing it," I probed.

"If he's interested, tell him to let me see his work."

"Okay, great," I said pumped, like a bicycle tire being filled with air.

"What were you telling him?" Hugo walked over and said to me once Principal Garner was gone.

"Oh my gosh. He's got a job for you!"

"A job for me? I'm not working for him. He's a jerk. You didn't need to make him think that. I was okay. He knows my situation, and thinks I'm a hoodrat. He can think whatever he likes."

"No, no, no. They're doing murals in the school. They're hiring an artist. You can get paid."

"What? You're trying to give me more charity like you did with your dad? I thought we talked about this, Ansli. If you can't accept poor, broke me, then what are we doing here? Always trying to make me come up and stuff."

"If you don't have any aspirations and think it's wrong for your girlfriend to try to help you when you're clearly probably better qualified than anybody they're considering, then you're right. What are we doing here?"

I walked the heck off. I was okay that he was going through, and I wasn't looking down on him. I just wasn't trying to be with a loser.

***

"Hey, wait up! Wait up! I didn't mean to be so cruel," Hugo caught up with me and said. "I don't want a girlfriend who is not satisfied with who I am."

"What's wrong with me being proud of who you are? My dad didn't get a chance to possibly be the mayor because he sat back and has been passive all his life. No, he went for his dreams. He networked. He met some of the right people. I'm learning how to be more like that because it's not inwardly in me like some of my sisters. I'm trying, but opportunities don't just always come. You have to go after them. Sometimes you have to be a little humble so you could convince the decision makers to give you a chance."

"So, what? I didn't handle the principal right?"

"Well ... no," I said when there was no other way to say it.

"I don't even know what to submit."

We got to my first class, and I saw that I had a substitute teacher. I just felt like I needed to get away and really help Hugo not blow this opportunity. I decided to do something crazy.

I turned to him and said, "I still have my set of keys. I know you've got some sketches, or we can work on something real quick that we can turn in."

"I don't want to get you in trouble like this. Skipping school? You're not even supposed to be driving your car. If your dad finds out you skipped school with me, he'll never really give me a chance."

"That's just a risk I'm willing to take. Besides I need your help with something."

"I need your help with something too," he said when we got to the car. He wouldn't go to the passenger side. Instead, he followed me over to the driver's door, threw my purse and backpack inside, and placed his lips on mine.

"We can't be gone too long. We need to hurry up and go. There're cameras in this parking lot."

"But you taste so good. I don't want to let you go," he said before kissing me again, this time with his tongue.

We went to the place where he was staying. He ran inside. My body so wanted to run in with him to finish what we started in the school parking lot, but I stayed put. Shortly, he came back out with some sketches and a worn art kit.

"I can show him these," he stated with pride.

Rightfully. The work I was looking at was stunning. I knew more about photography than drawing, but his lines, arches, coloring, and overall pieces were spectacular. He was talented.

"I'll sketch out a couple other things I'm thinking can go inside the school, but I'm not ready to go back just yet," he said to me as he stroked my cheek.

"Well, you sketch," I said, thinking I wanted to help my family. "I need your help anyway."

I couldn't remember all the turns I'd taken when I took Katera to the place she was staying. I didn't want to ask Hugo where I should be going because he was so into his work that he wasn't paying me any attention. I knew he would be mad at me if he knew what I was trying to do.

"This is it!" I said, finally excited.

"This is what? This is an abandoned warehouse."

"People stay here."

"I thought you were taking me someplace where you and I could have some fun."

"No," I told him. "I got my family into trouble, and I'm going to find the trouble and turn them in to the police."

"Did you hear me when I told you these people are dangerous?"

"But it's not night time. I've got to take some pictures and get the evidence. I did hear you. I can't go around accusing people when I'm not sure," I said.

Tire marks led all the way to some old storage units. I got out of my car against Hugo's wishes. Unfortunately, there was a padlock on the doors.

"We got to get back, or we're not going to make it in time for our next class. Come on, don't you hear the motorcycles?" he said.

We got in the car and drove off just before they could catch me snooping. Even with two big padlock storage units hiding what was behind the doors, I was certain it had our stuff and much more.

"Promise me you're not going to go over here anymore by yourself," Hugo said to me as we headed back to the school.

"I won't, but I've got to catch them when the garage is up."

"You got to let the police catch them when the garage is up. You're nobody's P.I., and you might think you're all inconspicuous, but you stick out around there. I don't want to be worried about you, too much else is going on, and I'm not trying to fight."

"Right," I said, grabbing one of his sketches. "So let's get back to the school, get this back to Dr. Garner, and get you this gig!"

He was grunting, and I didn't know what that was all about. I just wanted him to be excited and believe in himself as much as I did.

"What's wrong?" I asked him.

"I just don't want you to be disappointed in me if this doesn't work out."

With a smile, I said, "As long as you're trying, I can't be disappointed. I guess, in my mind, I see this working out way better than you can even dream of. Everyone is going to love your work. Trust me."

"Yeah, on the remote chance that he'll give me an opportunity, but whatever. I'll turn it in. I don't even have to worry about it. It's not like he's going to choose me."

"Oh, so you're saying if he does you're nervous?"

"We better hurry and get to class. We're late."

Hugo took me in a door I didn't even know existed. The halls were bare, but we hurried and got to our class. All was good. We skipped school, and no one was any the wiser until I actually got home where both of my parents were sitting there waiting on me. I knew that wasn't a good sign.

"Everybody get to work. Get busy with homework or something. Ansli, we need to see you right now in my office," my dad said, and he wasn't smiling.

I really didn't know how I was going to play this because I wasn't used to skipping school. Did he know what I'd done? Or, would I be playing myself if I just came out and admitted it and he didn't know? When I walked into my dad's office and saw this gentlemen whom I didn't know, who looked like somebody's secret service agent, I started freaking out.

"This is John Haynes. We hired him to keep an eye on you girls, and the report that I'm getting back for you is not a flattering one. Before he reads off the report is there something you'd like to tell us?" my dad asked, with my mom standing beside him.

John was about six feet, seven inches, and he wasn't a stick. He was thick and built like a brick. I didn't want to mess with him. I didn't want to prolong this, so I told the truth.

"I left school today."

"By yourself?" my mom asked.

"No, with Hugo."

"You left school with a boy?" my dad said.

"Yeah, but we didn't go and do what you think we went and did."

My mom looked at me like "Are you serious?" Her head was shaking, and my dad was tapping his foot. They weren't happy with me.

"No, seriously. If he was following us, then he should be able to tell you that I went to an abandoned warehouse."

"Oh, that's making me feel comfortable," my mom said.

"An abandoned warehouse, Ansli? What is wrong with you?" my dad uttered.

"Because, Dad, I think I know who took our stuff, and I think I know where they're holding it."

"And what? You were just going to try and retrieve it on your own? Why are you acting like this? Doing crazy stuff? Also, the girl that you had over here last weekend wasn't the only person you had in our house without our permission. This boy Hugo you're talking about, he came over then too. The choices you've made lately just don't make any sense. I know you've been angry about your parents, but you can't keep using that as an excuse. You're going to get yourself killed."

Sick and tired that they could not see I was trying to make things right, I said, "Okay, good. So what? If I'm not acting how a Sharp girl should act, maybe I need to leave here. Maybe you should call my grandparents. Maybe I need to go to England and live with them because no way am I acting like a girl who has your DNA. We are absolutely not at all alike."

CHAPTER SIX
AWESOME

"If that's the way you feel about it, Ansli, we'll try to get in touch with them," my dad said, looking as if I had snatched his heart from his chest and stomped on it.

I couldn't even look at my mom. I was trying to make things better. I cared about my folks, but here I was treating them as if their actions had caused me to put myself in harm's way. That wasn't fair, yet I didn't have the words to fix it, so I just left out.

"I ain't hear nothing break in there." Shelby quickly came up to me and joked as she escorted me to my room. "That's a good thing, right?"

My eyes rolled her way. I didn't feel like talking. She stayed beside me.

"How do I look?" Shelby asked.

"I dunno. You look cute. What?"

Shelby said, "Don't be irritable with me. You said you would help me. I got to take these pictures. I got to do it tonight because I got to send them to Spencer. He's gonna try to create this whole marketing campaign for me."

"You want me to take some pictures now? After I just got in trouble?"

"You didn't get in real trouble. They just went off a little bit, and you know they're only doing that because they care about you and love you so much."

"Shelby, quit being selfish. I'm not taking any pictures tonight."

Hotter than a whole bottle of chili peppers on nachos, Shelby said, "Whatever. You promised! You don't be selfish. If I could take the pictures of myself or get anybody else in this house to do them, I would."

"Calm down. I'm not trying to get into any more trouble."

"Then come snap a couple quick pictures. I'll set up a little background downstairs. Snap me quickly and we're done. Please ..."

"I said I'm not taking any daaa ..."

"You know what. Fine," Shelby said before I could even curse her out. "I don't know why I was even thinking about depending on you. Any and every time you need me to have your back, I always do it. I guess I just imagined you would give me the same courtesy. Regardless of what you were going through, you would understand this is business for me. I'm trying to give you an opportunity to shine. You're basically telling me to kiss your butt."

"I didn't ask to be a photographer," I declared.

"But you said you would try it. I see something in you."

It was the weirdest thing because, as she was talking to me, I realized this is probably how annoying I sounded to Hugo. He didn't see himself as a true artist—someone who could paint murals, make a difference in our school, and get some money for his work. I was pushing it down his throat because I could clearly see him shining in that arena. Here was my sister, basically doing the same thing. Granted, she'd benefit if my pictures turned out to be worth anything. She thought they were going to be fabulous. Why was I giving her a hard time?

"Go on downstairs, don't work yourself up. I'll take the pictures," I uttered.

"You will? For real?" she said with glee, as she jumped up and down like she'd won the lottery. "Thanks, Ansli. I really need this. Your pictures are going to be beautiful too!" Off my sister went.

Slone was coming towards me, headed towards the kitchen to get something to eat. With attitude, she said, "Don't let Shelby break your camera."

"Why are you always so freaking negative?" I said to her, really fed up with her smart mouth.

"Why do you keep everything all bottled up inside?"

"Well, I ain't bottling it up now. You talk too much."

"You get mad at our parents because they don't tell you things, but when people tell you what they think, you get mad that they told you. I mean, you can't have it both ways, Ansli. The world ain't picture perfect."

She had a great point. I was mad at so many when I really needed to look within myself. My dad loved saying "you never know what you look like until you get your picture taken." My sister Sloan hadn't gotten a camera and taken a snapshot, but she'd certainly called me out. Now I clearly could see that I had issues that needed to be fixed.

"I love you, Ansli, and I say what I say because I care. Skipping school, bringing people over here when Mom and Dad aren't here, that's not you. It takes a special person to be respectful and do what they're told, and I've always admired you for that. You've done that with such grace. Now you've changed in a bad way. I am who I am, and I make no apologies for it, but you aren't who you were, and I think you're making a mistake." Sloan patted me on the shoulder and went on to the kitchen.

Without even thinking I turned right around and went back into my dad's study. "I owe you guys an apology. I'm sorry."

My mom was looking out the window. She couldn't even look my way. I knew for them that my actions, not my words were going to move them. Though they did deserve an apology, and I was glad I gave it, I knew I was going to have to show them that I was real. That I was serious and that I was sorry.

Before I could leave my dad said, "And we know where this warehouse is located. We've got people on it. Don't go back there again. Am I making myself clear?"

"Yes, sir."

I went to my room and grabbed some of my equipment. When I went downstairs, I was amazed. Shelby was serious about this photo shoot. On one wall she put up some hot pink fabric. On another wall there was a black background, and another was white. She was ready to go. She was posing like she was a model. I took a few pictures that way, but she said this was a business and that the pictures needed to be professional. So while she could have some that were fun, she also needed some that were firm.

"Yeah, this one is good. Smile, stand over to the left. Give me a little more attitude." Before I knew it, I was all into it.

"What are you girls doing down here?" my mom said about an hour later.

"I just had a photo shoot thanks to Ansli," Shelby announced.

My mom asked, "Can I see the pictures?"

"You're gonna love them," Shelby said before even seeing them herself.

Thankful for my sister's belief in me, I hooked the camera into my computer and pulled up a ton of images. Shelby was so excited. She loved every image. When my mom smiled at me, I realized I done good, and that felt great.

***

September was flying by. I had gone a couple weeks with no incident. I was studying. I was obeying all my parents' rules. I wasn't all into Hugo. I was researching what a photographer needs to have for a successful business.

Shelby's marketing campaign came out so well. Everyone she showed the pictures to wanted to have some done by the same person, and that person was me. While I wanted to know more about my biological dad's state of mind the last day he and my mom were on Earth, I wished my maternal grandparents were in my life. I didn't want to feel upset that my parents kept me in the dark for so long. I realized if I took that energy and channeled it into this whole photography business, then I'd be really doing something.

Once I was going to class, and I got stopped by Freddie and Val, two of the homeless kids I met with a couple weeks back.

"Hey, y'all. How's it going?"

"Oh, so you just gonna *hey* us like it's no big deal? Like you didn't make us a lot of promises that you haven't been keeping?"

"I'm sorry. I know I told you guys I was going to get with you. I had every intention to do so. It's just been so crazy. A lot's going on with my family..."

"Yeah, yeah, yeah, we know," Val said.

"We see y'all on TV sometimes."

I guessed I looked a little funny like, "Y'all have a TV?" but I didn't mean to do that. I didn't mean to make any assumptions. I told them I was going to go where they lived, but I hadn't been there. They could live in a palace for all I knew. I did need to go to the foster home.

"I'm sorry. How can I make it up to you guys?" I asked.

"We don't want your help," Freddie said.

Val added, "Yeah you were probably doing it just for show to impress the principal or something."

Squinting, I said, "I wasn't trying to impress the principal."

"We seen you cut class. You ain't as goody-two-shoes as you try to make it out to be," Freddie said.

"No, I've got a lot going on. That's what I'm trying to tell you guys. But I do care, and I do want to help."

"Whatever," Val said, as they turned around to walk away.

"No, seriously. What can I do?"

"The man the state put in charge to run the group home shouldn't be there," Val came back and said. "If you just meet him, maybe you can figure out what to do to help us."

"Okay, I'm on it," I said, meaning every word.

Val finally smiled, "Great so when can you come? Today? Tomorrow?"

Needing to settle her expectations, I said, "No, I was thinking in a couple weeks. I'm on punishment. I don't even have a car."

"Oh, see. Freddie's right. You're full of it," Val angrily hissed like a mad snake before she walked away.

"Girl, you better hurry up and get to class," my sister Shelby said, passing me with Spencer.

Seeing them changed my frown to a smile. She was all in love, and that was so adorable. I liked the way they looked at each other.

"You took some real nice pictures," Spencer said.

"I hear you've done a real nice brochure on her," I replied.

"I'll show it to you later. I'm so excited, I won't have anything to do after school today. You wanna ride home with me?" Shelby asked.

"Spencer, can I talk to my sister for a minute?" I said to him, thinking of a way to rectify a situation.

"Yeah sure," he said to me.

Spencer leaned over and gave Shelby a kiss on the cheek. She looked like she did not want him to leave. That did make me long for Hugo. They were a cute couple.

"What's up?" Shelby asked.

"I need you to take me somewhere."

"I'm not going to no warehouse thing or whatever Dad told you you're not supposed to go to."

"No, it's nothing like that. Public service. Maybe a place where you can do another fashion show and get some publicity for it. Or maybe a place we can take Dad back to help with his campaign."

"Where is this place?"

"I'll tell you after school."

"Then I'm not saying yes 'til I know. You are not tricking me, Ansli. You done gone all renegade on me. I'm always down for a cause, but after getting mixed up in the whole domestic violence thing—being at Sydnee's and being scared of being shot when her crazy fiancé came with a gun —I'm taking a few steps back."

"You wouldn't even have the brochure if it wasn't for me. You gonna do me like that? You think I would put us in harm's way? Really?"

Shelby looked at me. "That's true. Alright, after school, but we can't stay long wherever this is though."

After school when I walked to the car with Freddie and Val, my sister was narrowing her eyes. But I introduced them to each other and just said that they needed a ride home.

When we pulled up on the group home's property, everything looked kosher, on the up and up, and really nice. Then we met Mr. Ron Wheeler. He was a redhead with a receding hair line.

At first, he was snappy. "I don't have no

papers on y'all! You can't be staying here. We full to capacity." But when Val explained who we were, who our father was, his tone changed.

"Oh, well I need more money. Maybe your dad can help the city come off on some more. These children don't have enough."

"What do you mean they don't have enough?" my sister asked, doing what I knew she'd do—care.

Mr. Wheeler laughed, "Just teasing. Y'all stay as long as you want now you hear."

When the cost was clear, Val tugged on my sister's arm and said, "He's serious. We don't get enough. We barely get enough helpings. He doesn't buy a lot of groceries, and when there is food, he stocks it in his room. He thinks we don't know, but we know."

My sister came up with a plan that they'd show me. So she went into the next room and kept Mr. Wheeler company. I went around with Val and Freddie taking pictures of all the things that were out of place. It seemed as if Mr. Wheeler was really shady, taking money that was supposed to go to the group home and spending it on himself. He drove a nice car when the bathrooms were clogged. He had a bunch of nice clothes when the air conditioner was broken. He had the finest furniture in his bedroom, but the bunk beds that the kids were sleeping on barely seemed to be staying together. Yeah, this man was shady, and my camera held all of the evidence.

***

When Shelby and I got home, we immediately went to find my dad. Thankfully he was nestled in his office, strategizing with his campaign manager. But like a great dad, when he saw us coming, he asked his strategist for a second of privacy to talk to his girls.

"Go on, Ansli, you tell him."

"No, no, no you tell him," I said, knowing Shelby had the passion and could always articulate best what we needed to get our parents to respond.

"There is this group home where a bunch of kids from our school live, and the guy who is running it is a crook."

"Please explain."

And so we did and showed him the pictures too. At the end of it, my dad was livid.

"See girls, these are the things in the city that I want to know about that are wrong. I can't change stuff if people hide things from us. We put people in place to do right by the citizens. I'll be looking into this some more."

"Looking into this some more?" I said a little heated.

"Not because I don't believe you girls or don't think you have enough evidence, but just let me do some digging. Tell your friends to hold tight."

"Okay."

I just shook my head, got up, and walked out. I knew my dad wasn't the mayor yet, but at first I didn't want him to be because I thought it would be too much attention and spotlight on the family. But the more I was growing and the more I was getting involved in my own community, I realized that we needed a good leader like him who truly cared. There was too much corruption around us. The only way the corruption could be stopped is if someone with the right heart was at the helm. But how was I going to go and call Freddie and Val to tell them to hold on and that my dad was on it? I had no details and could not tell them what kind of change would be brought and when? They needed something different to happen immediately, but I had no time frame. That was frustrating.

Later, my sisters Slade, Sloan, and Yuri came into my room. Sloan said, "So you want to be a photographer, huh?"

"I do," I said, finally owning it.

"We have a job you can bid for," Slade said.

"What's that mean?" I asked.

Sloan, Miss-Know-It-All, stepped up and said, "Bidding is when you submit your resume with everybody else's, but in this case you might be the only one who submits."

"Submits for what?" I questioned.

"Our homecoming week got moved to the game coming up. Since we're a new school, it can't be later like normal. The school is having a hard time trying to find somebody to be the photographer. The principal just sent out an e-mail asking that if we knew anyone to have him or her contact the school."

"This could be perfect," I said. "Val and Freddie and some of the others need a job, I can split the profits with them. I would just need to cover the cost for the materials and buy the photo paper. But backgrounds, lights, stands, and everything else I got that here. Thank you guys!"

My sisters were confused about whom I was talking about, but were still so excited. Actually, I was excited as well.

Shelby rushed in through the bathroom and immediately pulled out a bunch of clothes from my closet. "You got to have a photo shoot."

"I'm the photographer, what are you talking about?"

Shelby insisted, "You're going to show me how to hold a camera. I'm going to snap a couple pictures of you, we're going to send it over to Spencer, and he's ready to design you some business cards and some price packages so when you go in tomorrow morning and you meet with Mr. Garner, you'll be ready to go."

"But what's it going to be called?" Slade said.

"Ansli Photography," Yuri uttered with excitement, as we all were shocked by the quiet sister's comment.

"I can help you with the write up explaining what your company is and why you should have it. And why don't you call Hugo? Get him to sketch a logo he can send over. Or Spencer can do something on the computer. Your choice," Shelby said, committed to developing my brand.

"But quick, we've got to get busy."

Working with the four of them felt so great. Somehow we came up with aqua and black as my colors. The picture we settled on was me holding my camera and just half of my face. It was such a cool image. Ansli Photography had it going on. And I didn't want to bug Hugo because he was so busy coming up with mural designs to show, that I just let Spencer choose me something. What he sent over captured everything I was thinking.

My sisters were so excited to show my mom what we designed when she came home. When she called me into her bedroom, I didn't know what she was going to think. Our relationship had been a little estranged. We could always talk about everything, but over the last few weeks, we hadn't talked about anything. Yet there I was, a daughter really seeking her mother's permission to carry out a dream.

"I'm sorry I didn't ask you about all this before we dived into it, but I want you to like it," I honestly uttered, showing her the design.

She smiled and said, "If you like it, I love it. I'm proud of you, and I know you're going to do a good job."

Three days later, it was actually homecoming. I had gotten the gig. Freddie and Val were working for me, and everyone loved the pictures Ansli Photography took. I was in my element, making sure I was helping everyone else look beautiful. The feeling of seeing my business come to fruition, going from a dream to a reality, felt awesome.

CHAPTER SEVEN
ADORABLE

Between my sisters, Freddie, Val and other help-
ers, my first night of business went off without
a hitch. Everybody got receipts for the money
they paid. In this world of social media—in ad-
dition to taking down their information—I also
had a box to check if they would allow me to
post their picture on my Instagram page for
Ansli Photography. Shelby made sure everyone
checked it. With a school of over 3,000, I took
1,672 pictures. I was getting tons of likes because everyone wanted to check out everyone
else's photo and, of course, see his or her own.

The comments were uplifting.

"Ansli, you are so good at this. Keep it up!"

"Where have you been all my life, Ansli Sharp? You make me look good."

"Ansli, your prices rock! Everybody else just be rippin' us off for bad pictures."

"Go Ansli! You make the ugly people look good."

"I hope Ansli Photography is doing prom."

"Could you cover my sweet-sixteen party?"

"Ansli Sharp, could you give me the number of the guy who's in picture fifteen?"

I couldn't stop looking at the comments. Even the next week in class I went from just being one of the Sharp sisters to having my own identity. People wanted to be my friend. People told me I inspired them to pursue their passions. It was unreal, but it was real at the same time. I wasn't even paying attention, and I didn't even see Katera in my classroom talking to my teacher until my name was called.

My teacher said, "Ansli, someone wants to see you outside."

The girl had been missing in action for

a week. There were so many people I had on the lookout for her, but she was nowhere to be found. Now she was trying to find me? What the heck was up with her?

"What do you want, Katera?" I said with big attitude when we were alone in the hall.

"I just want you to hear me out."

Agitated, I huffed, "I let you stay at my house so you can rest, shower, and be safe. You have somebody steal from my family, and you want me to hear you out? Where were you when the cops came? Where have you been the last week? Why do you think I want to hear from you now?"

"Because I need to apologize."

"What? You want me to be sympathetic to you again? Bring you over my house so y'all can steal the new things we had to replace? You've got the wrong fool. You already had me once, and shame on you for taking advantage of someone trying to be your friend. I cared."

"I know, but I was forced into doing it. When you saw me the Friday before last, and I had that black eye, I didn't show you these."

Katera pulled up her sleeve and showed me three little circle marks on her hands.

Mortified, I asked, "Are those burns?"

"Yep, from a cigarette. I was forced to do what I did, bullied by these guys. They break you off a little piece of money, I guess to eat. To have the lady you met, Momma Dee, not be tortured, I did what they said. It took a lot of friends to save my tail, but even after I did that, they still roughed me up when we got home."

I was really falling for what Katera was telling me. I didn't want too, but I had no choice. As mad as I was at her, now my heart was pounding in agony hearing all that she was enduring.

Katera voiced, "And I can't take it anymore. I can't watch them hurt anyone anymore. I want to turn them in."

I never even imagined a few weeks ago that anything could be worse than domestic violence. Hearing the stories Shelby told me of Spencer's mom being abused by her husband, of the Sydnee Sheldon designer being abused by her fiancé, and of one of the high school girls taking physical assaults from her boyfriend. But just pure violence was way worse, and it needed to be stopped. I yelled into the classroom that I was going to the office, and the teacher shook his head.

"We're here to see Principal Garner," I said to the secretary.

"Do you have a pass from your teacher?"

"My teacher said it was okay," I said, trying to hold my composure.

I know she was just doing her job, but we were in the office during a class period. Whether we had a pass or not, if we were in here to see the principal, it was important. We didn't need to be blocked.

"Well, my rules are, if you don't have a pass . . ."

Katera hit the desk. "Sometimes you need to use common sense and bend the rules before you get fired."

"What's going on out here?" the principal came out and said.

"We need to see you, sir, it's pretty important," I said.

"Well, you didn't say it was pretty important," the secretary said.

Katera put her hand up in front of the lady's face.

"I need you to call my dad, sir," I said when we got into his office.

Without hesitation Mr. Garner did. My father was there in about forty minutes with the police. They took down my statement about the warehouse I said I knew about. Katera gave details about two other warehouses. She named people but told the police that she wanted to be anonymous because she was scared for her life. When I was about to tell what they had done to her, she kicked me in the shin.

"That's all they need to know right now. The rest is private," she said, letting me know without actually telling me that I didn't need to say anything.

My father and Mr. Garner thanked her for her strength. Later that night on the news my dad was credited for bringing down a big stolen goods ring as four suspects were being hauled off to jail.

"If I was the Mayor of the good city of Charlotte, I vow to you that we're going to help our homeless citizens so that they never have to feel bullied or pressured into turning to crime."

My dad didn't just talk about change. He was about change. His caring spirit warmed my heart.

***

"Thank you, Daddy, for coming," I said as we pulled up at the group home where Freddie and Val lived.

My dad didn't come with press and cameras, he came with difference makers. He brought the sheriff and the director of Children and amily Services for the state. They were coming to investigate the claims that I'd alleged.

"I can't believe that you're really here," Val said as she opened the door and let me in with the important looking entourage.

"I'm Ansli's father, Mr. Sharp," my dad explained.

"He's an attorney," I said.

"And I understand you guys have been taken advantage of in this group home. I've brought some people with me who can correct that.

Who else is here with you guys?"

"A few others who live here and the assistant lady in charge. Mr. Wheeler is gone, but he should be back in any minute," Freddie said.

"Well, let's get busy," the sheriff said. "Let's take some statements. If there is anyone else here who wants to let us know what's been going on, tell them to come down now."

All nine students who lived in the house and the assistant counselor came down to tell all. Freddie started, "When we get our checks from social security, or wherever people get checks from, we have to give some to Mr. Wheeler."

"What for?" the director asked.

Another teen who lived there piped in and said, "What's it not for? Toilet tissue, getting our clothes washed, water for baths . . . anything we need, he's making us pay for it."

"Why hasn't anyone reported it?" the assistant counselor said, looking surprised herself. "I didn't know all that was going on until a couple weeks ago. A lot of teens came up and complained. I just got placed here, and once I started questioning Wheeler, he told me if I asked too many questions I wouldn't have a job."

Freddie said, "That's basically what he said to us. If we complained about paying, there is a list of kids waiting to get in here that would. I've been on the streets. I know how hard it is. The last place I wanted to go back to was being truly homeless. It's one thing not to have parents, but at least we're sort of a family. Even though the person who is supposed to be over us is completely taking advantage of us, I've got a few brothers and sisters here, and it's more than what I had when I was on my own. If I have to give a few of the pennies the government gives me to keep it, then that's just what I've been doing."

"You shouldn't have to do that," my father said.

"Well, I see here that we've been sending him money to fix certain things in this house," the director told us as he reviewed files in his hands.

"That's another problem," Freddie said. "He's got a new car, some new clothes, expensive cologne and everything else, but ain't nothing been repaired around here. We can take a tour, and I can show you right now stuff that's still broke. If he told you it's been fixed, he's lying."

The director held up a photo of the stove door attached. "He sent us pictures of stuff being fixed."

"I don't know how," Freddie said as he motioned for us to check things out for ourselves.

We all followed Freddie. "See, the stove is broken." The door fell right off of it. "In the pantry there is hardly any food. The toilet upstairs is broken. It was so hot in here, but now that fall is here, it's no use to even getting the A/C."

When we were finished with the tour, the adults were seething with anger. The timing was perfect because Mr. Wheeler was walking in the door. He had the audacity to say, "The cops are here! Oh, my gosh. Which one of these kids did something? Mr. Director, hello! I have my assistant counselor here because I know I'm not supposed to leave the kids unsupervised, but she should be here. She's here, right? Freddie, what did you guys do?"

"They're hungry. What time is dinner?" the director asked.

"Well, with all due respect, sir, I need to find out why the cops are here and find out why they got in trouble then I'll get them fed. These kids are resilient. I'm sure they cleaned out the pantry eating all the snacks."

"If you knew the pantry was empty, why didn't you fill it back up?" the director questioned.

"I was on my way to, but I got a text message that said the cops were here."

"Really, could I see your phone?" the director asked.

Mr. Wheeler was dark as a tire, but he was turning as red as ketchup. He looked at me. "I know you. You-you don't live here."

I said, "I told you I'd bring my father back."

"Yeah, did we have an appointment? Did I miss something?" Mr. Wheeler said.

Coldly my dad said, "I wouldn't help you even if I won the lottery."

"I don't understand. What have these kids told you about me?" Mr. Wheeler started to panic.

"Arrest him, Sherriff," the director said.

"Mr. Wheeler, come with us, please," the sheriff said, stepping forward, cuffs in hand.

He didn't want to go calmly, but when the director started reading off the list of violations, he finally surrendered and was hauled away. The assistant counselor whom Freddie and Val liked was appointed to the newly opened position. They got the key to director's bedroom that he kept locked up, and soon as we went inside, there were tons of food and money, and there was even a new stove purchased, but it had not been installed.

My dad and the director took time to talk to all the kids, finding out what they needed, what their dreams and goals were, and trying to find ways to help them succeed. I don't know how the press found out what was going on. Once the news channels got there, and with the director of Children and Family Services singing my father's praises for cracking another case, my dad was interviewed.

He didn't take any of the credit though. He said, "I've got a daughter who cares, and I encourage all parents to listen to their children. We might want to protect them and keep them away from things we think will hurt them, but they're stronger and more resilient than we know."

My dad hugged me. I truly felt his love. With cameras flashing all around me, I realized that was a moment I wanted to keep forever.

***

I had never been more proud of a person than I was watching Hugo unveil the mural that he had done in the front hallway. Our principal let him do one to see how it went. The school board, local principals, some parents, and student leaders who were invited to the unveiling were all clapping at the magnificent creation that Hugo had done in two days.

My dad didn't even tell me where we were going after church. Hugo had asked him to make it a surprise, and I thought since it was my birthday, my parents were trying to do something special for me. After all, I was turning eighteen. Seeing Hugo's creation was better than any scrumptious dinner ever could be.

"And see, I didn't want this young man to do it. I'm just going to go ahead and admit it," Mr. Garner said, being completely honest. "That's why you gotta listen to these young people. He didn't want to charge me anything just to give him a chance to do something, and he had a great point. We could have painted over it if I hated it, but the board and I have decided that we want you to do the other two murals. I think you're going to like the amount you're going to be paid."

He whispered something in Hugo's ear. My boyfriend got ecstatic. Everyone wanted to congratulate him.

People were mixing and mingling, and Hugo's mom came over to me and said, "Thank you for helping my son. Not many help us, but you always believed in him. Thank you for caring about my son. I've always known he had talent, but seeing him actually doing it is better than anything I could have dreamed. I'm going to go back to school myself. I'm going to make something of me because Hugo shown me the way, and you've shown him the way. Bless you young girl."

My father talked some to his mom. My sisters talked to Hugo. Spencer was even there and told him how proud of him he was. I couldn't say the two of them would be best buds, but now Hugo had money to take us out to dinner, and I could see he was proud.

My mom came over to me and gave me a big hug, but her eyes were teary, and I didn't understand. "What's wrong?"

"It's your birthday. We've gotten you the gift we think you want," she said, gripping me tighter.

After all the cake and punch at the school, we were back to my house. My momma catered the dinner, and, yes, I liked to eat good, but it was more Yuri's style with seven-course meals and all, but then two people whom I didn't know came from out of nowhere. They were an elderly white couple. They were smiling my way, but I didn't know them.

"We've got your grandparents here from England, Ansli," my mom said.

"Hello, gorgeous," my grandmother said with watery eyes.

It was weird because I'd longed to connect with them, but actually having them there felt strange, like I didn't know them at all.

"I just wanted to come. I owe you an apology. Your grandpa wanted to take you when our precious daughter was killed. I didn't. After what had gone on with your dad and our daughter we just ... I just ... " And then she broke down crying. "When the Sharps told us you wanted to live with us, I figured maybe this is my chance to get it right. This is my chance to make up for not having you in my life all these years; you and your sister. Looking at you and your sister, I can see our daughter."

Now I knew why my parents didn't tell me everything. I would've been heartbroken knowing not only did my dad take my mom's life, but also knowing that my maternal grandparents didn't want anything to do with us. Who could blame the Sharps for keeping it all and not telling us every painful detail? Looking into my parent's eyes and seeing them both emotional, I knew that I was home. I rushed over and kissed and hugged my mom and dad. I didn't want to go anymore. I owed the Sharps a big "I'm sorry." I was thankful.

"You want to stay with us?" my mom cried.

"We thought we owed it to you to get you your grandparents," my dad said.

"And I hope they stay in my life," I said.

"We will, but if you want to stay here, we'll understand," my grandmother replied.

"They're all I've ever known as parents, and they love me and Yuri, and they've given us the world. If we could come visit some this summer, that would be great, but I want to live here."

"Good, because you were going by yourself!" Yuri yelled out.

The doorbell rang. It was Hugo and his mom. Shelby went to go pick them up.

He came right over to me and said, "I'm glad you pushed me to follow my dreams. I never would've known people would like my art unless you would've gotten on me."

"Awe, isn't that cute," Shelby said.

"Well, I owe you the same kind of talk," I said to my sister before she could get away. "Had you not pushed me to be a photographer, I wouldn't be following my goals either."

It was good to be able to admit shortcomings; to look in the mirror, to understand on a birthday your strengths and your weaknesses and figure out a way to get better. I'd taken my parents through a lot, but they loved me anyhow, and regardless of what my biological dad did to my mom way back then, I didn't have any of those tendencies. Besides who knew all of the stuff that he was dealing with to make him do what he did?

It was my birthday. A time to celebrate, and before we sat down to eat, I set up my camera and got my family and friends close so that we could take a group picture. When the camera snapped and they all wanted to see how they looked, I realized we were perfect—better than what they could have imagined. Whether my dad won the upcoming election or not, we were a unit that cared about each other and our community.

If I could speak to teens out there who're scared to go after their dreams, I would encourage them to think about their goals day and night and go after them with their whole heart. Whatever they're imagining, once they get it, it's going to be so much better and for sure worth it. I was living proof of that. On my eighteenth birthday, with all I had been dealing with, my life was okay. And the picture of me standing with my family and friends turned out to be adorable.

ACKNOWLEDGMENTS

Thanks to everyone who makes my work better:

To my parents, Dr. Franklin and Shirley Perry, thank you for telling me that I could do anything I dreamed of.

To my publisher, especially, Andrew Karre, thank you for catching my vision.

To my extended family, thank you for your support which helps me to keep working.

To my assistants Shaneen Clay, Alyxandra Pinkston, and Candace Johnson, thank you for being so on top of things and helping bring what's in my head to paper.

To my dear friends, thank you for your friendship which makes me a better person.

To my teens, Dustyn, Sydni, and Sheldyn, thank you for working hard so that all your dad and I envision for you is becoming possible.

To my husband, Derrick, thank you for being my everything.

To my readers, thank you for trying out my work that hopefully will bless you.

And to my Heavenly Father, thank you for getting me to a new company that believes in my work and is helping me reach more young people for You.

ABOUT THE AUTHOR

STEPHANIE PERRY MOORE is the author of more than sixty young adult titles, including the Grovehill Giants series, the Lockwood Lions series, the Payton Skky series, the Laurel Shadrach series, the Perry Skky Jr. series, the Yasmin Peace series, the Faith Thomas Novelzine series, the Carmen Browne series, the Morgan Love series, the Alec London series, and the Beta Gamma Pi series. Mrs. Moore is a motivational speaker who enjoys encouraging young people to achieve every attainable dream. She lives in the greater Atlanta area with her husband, Derrick, and their three children. Visit her website at www.stephanieperrymoore.com.

THE **SHARP** SISTERS

Make Something of It

Better Than Picture Perfect

Turn Up for Real

Truth and Nothing But

Icing on the Cake